# REDEMPTION

Harish Vasudevan lives in Bangalore with his family. This is his first book.

# HARISH VASUDEVAN

# REDEMPTION

First published by Westland Books, a division of Nasadiya Technologies Private Limited, in 2024

No. 269/2B, First Floor, 'Irai Arul', Vimalraj Street, Nethaji Nagar, Alapakkam Main Road, Maduravoyal, Chennai 600095

Westland and the Westland logo are the trademarks of Nasadiya Technologies Private Limited, or its affiliates.

Copyright © Harish Vasudevan, 2024

Harish Vasudevan asserts the moral right to be identified as the author of this work.

ISBN: 9789360450175

10 9 8 7 6 5 4 3 2 1

This is a work of fiction. Names, characters, organisations, places, events and incidents are either products of the author's imagination or used fictitiously.

All rights reserved

Typeset by Jojy Philip, New Delhi

Printed at Nutech Print Services, India

No part of this book may be reproduced, or stored in a retrieval system, or transmitted in any form or by any means, electronic, mechanical, photocopying, recording, or otherwise, without express written permission of the publisher.

*To the survivors*

# Part 1

# 1

Archana and Raju stand holding hands, watching the sun dip ever lower on the horizon, over the Agara lake. The sky's colours shift from vivid oranges and reds to the gentle purples and blues of twilight. The air is still and peaceful, the cool air carrying faint sounds from a village a few kilometres away.

Raju pulls Archana closer to him, feeling a shared warmth and contentment spread through his body. He kisses the top of her head, breathing in the scent of her hair. After years of marriage, he still loves her with a fierce intensity.

This evening, beneath an orange sky, they look like a normal middle-class couple. There is no way for them to know what the future holds.

Archana looks up at her husband, her eyes shining with love and admiration. She remembers the first time she met him, nineteen years ago, when he came home with his parents to 'see' her.

He was not handsome in the conventional sense but he had a kind face and a ready smile. He did little things that made her comfortable during that performance she had to put up in front of her prospective in-laws. At the time, she had no idea how their life together would turn out. Now, held fast in his arms, she allows herself to feel grateful.

As the last rays of the sun disappear, Archana and Raju turn towards home. The streets are bustling with life and energy; the smell of spices and the aroma of freshly cooked street food fill the air. They hold hands to ensure neither gets lost or waylaid by a street vendor. Every few steps, they have to veer around someone squatting on the pavement, selling vegetables or snacks.

'Do you want something to eat?' he asks, in Kannada.

'Let's get some onion pakoras packed. We can have them with dinner,' she replies.

While he is buying the pakoras, Archana stops at a small roadside Ganesha temple to say a quick prayer. Anyone looking at her would have seen a woman of medium height with black hair open to her waist, a bright red bindi on the forehead. Today she is wearing a green checked Madurai cotton sari with an orange blouse. Short prayer complete, she bends and touches her fingers to the feet of the deity three times before reaching for some vermilion to mark her forehead.

'Come, let's go,' says Raju.

'One second, let me get some flowers from the puja for Shalu. I know she has been studying really hard, but we need God to be on her side too.'

Shalu, or Shalini, is their only child.

They had decided early on that they would not have any more children. The reasoning was simple: they would be able to give her all that she wanted without having to worry about setting anything aside for another child. They were also not among those who would do anything to have a boy. But it took some convincing, and moving towns, to get their parents off their backs after Shalu was born.

'Why can't you have another child? It could be a boy.'

'What if we have another girl?'

'Well, you can always try again.'

They soon realised this was a futile conversation and stopped discussing the matter altogether. There followed a period of distance and silence before the need to spend time with their granddaughter brought everyone to the table. And Shalu's kind, sensitive nature quickly healed any cracks that had appeared.

The move to Bangalore was good for all of them. Shalu got into a good school. Archana landed a job with one of the top IT companies and progressed rapidly up the ladder. Given his expertise in finance, Rajesh was also snapped up by one of the larger private companies. They soon settled into a routine that included regular catch-ups with a very small group of good friends.

Shalu developed an equally tight-knit group of her own. They hung out every day and talked about school and teachers, and the latest shows and music concerts. And, of course, crushes. This was the age, wasn't it?

'Will Shalu be home?' asks Rajesh as they make their way through the winding streets and turn into the narrow lane that leads to their apartment block.

'She's gone out to meet some friends and relax for a while. I am sure they've all been studying all day.'

'Exams start on Monday, right? I'll drop her off to school. She can come back with Tabassum or one of her other friends.'

'She would love that,' says Archana. 'And you can help calm her before the exam.'

In a few minutes Raju is opening the door to their third-floor apartment. He hangs the keys on a little bird stand that already holds a multitude of miscellaneous keys.

'Let me check my email and then go for a bath,' Archana says. 'I have a few calls later tonight. Shalu should be back by then as well. Dinner at nine? Will you be ok till then?'

'Yes, don't worry. I'll catch up with the newspapers. Didn't have much time this morning.'

Rajesh pours himself a glass of water as Archana disappears into their bedroom that also serves as her office. He goes into the living room, taking in the familiar furniture and the smell of home. As he settles down with the newspaper, his mind wanders to Shalu and her upcoming exams. He knows how hardworking she is and how seriously she takes her studies. Sometimes, too seriously.

Lost in thought, he doesn't hear the door open and close. It's only when he sees Shalu standing in front of him, a tired look on her face, that he realises she is home.

'Hey, what's wrong?' he asks, setting aside the newspaper. Though their mother tongue is Kannada, Archana insists on conversing in English at home so that Shalu has no trouble speaking it at school.

Shalu sits down next to him, her head on his shoulder. 'It's nothing, really. Just exam stress, I guess. Always feels like there's so much more to be done.'

Rajesh puts an arm around her. 'Sini, don't worry so much about it. Do your best. Revise with your friends. The rest is out of your hands.'

When Shalu was a baby, she couldn't say her full name, only Sini. And that remained her father's name for her.

'I know,' she says, her voice muffled.

'Why don't you relax for a bit? Have a bath, listen to some music, and by 9 o'clock Amma will be ready for dinner.'

'I think I'll do that. Exams start next week, so I can't relax too much, you know. If I don't do well, you and Amma will be the first to scold me,' she says with a half-smile.

'That's true.' He smiles back at her. 'Very important, these exams. They'll decide your future, so you have no choice but to do well. But it's important that you don't stress about them. I know you'll do well. The mid-terms and mocks were excellent, right? So just go now and take a break. See you at dinner!'

## 2

Come Monday, Shalu and Raju are ready to head out to the exam centre while Archana stands at the door with a silver plate on which is placed a small stone image of Saraswati, the goddess of learning, a little silver lamp, and some vibhuti. After a short prayer, father and daughter head out of the door.

This will be their routine for the next two weeks. All socialising is paused. No television or other distractions are allowed while Shalu's exams are ongoing. And suddenly, just like that, they are on the penultimate day.

'Shalu, come on! We're waiting for you for dinner,' Archana calls out. It's past 9 p.m. in the Gowda household. A little later than usual. They usually try to finish eating by nine, so they can watch something on TV together. But these past two weeks, everything has been subservient to Shalu's schedule.

'Just a minute, Amma. One last section and then I am done,' Shalu calls from behind the closed door.

'Tomorrow is her last exam?' asks Raju.

'Yes. Physics. Her least favourite subject.'

'I didn't much care for physics either. Had to cram the answer to every question,' Raju laughs, thinking back to his college days.

'Oh, I liked it a lot. That's how I got into electronics and then computers.'

'I was more of a numbers person. I told you, no, my father wanted me to be a CA like him and his brother. I was never clever enough for that, so I became an accountant. Once I joined though, I found I liked the sense of order in accounting. There are sets of rules. Just follow them and all is well. Everyone knows the same rules, so there's no scope for confusion—unless you don't know the rules, of course. Very predictable. I liked that.'

He turns to Archana. 'You know how Shalu has been talking about studying aviation after school? Still the same, you think? No change?'

'Well, that's what she's been saying consistently for a few months now. Sounds to me like she is serious.'

'Let's talk it over with her this weekend. I need to know how much money will be needed. Maybe we'll have to take a loan.' Raju's practical mind swings into action.

'Yes. Let's do that. Also, don't forget we have Prasad and Janet coming for dinner on Saturday.'

'Of course I remember. Should be a fun evening. I know they started off as your friends but I like them a lot, unlike some of your other classmates,' Rajesh laughs. 'Ok, now I'm really starving. Can we please eat?'

'SHALU. We are starting.'

'Sorry, sorry. Here I am,' Shalu says, arriving breathless at the table. 'I am so nervous. Tomorrow is the last exam, you know, and it's the one subject I hate.'

The lines on Raju's face soften as he smiles down at his daughter. His eyes sparkle with pride; she is a smart and confident young woman. Raju can never be angry with her for long—one look from those glittering black eyes melts away any rage that burns within him. He knows he will do everything in his power to protect her from the world.

Shalu serves herself rice, sambar and her favourite bhindi fry and settles down with her plate. 'How was your day, Amma?'

'Oh, you know. Budgets, appraisals, all the usual boring stuff. But then, we were briefed on a really interesting new project. You saw that Apple launched a new phone two months ago? It's called the iPhone. Very fancy phone. No buttons. Everything on a touchscreen. I can't see how anyone will use it, it's so expensive. What if it falls? That glass screen will break immediately.'

She sits back and continues thoughtfully, 'Nokia and Motorola pretty much have the market covered.

At work, of course, everyone will continue to use the BlackBerry. But Gary, my boss who has just joined us from AT&T, is very excited and is going around telling everyone that the iPhone will change the way we use mobile phones. Apparently, we won't use computers so much, we'll soon be downloading something called applications through which we can do anything at all. Can you believe that?'

Raju and Shalini exchange glances. It's not often that Archana leads the conversation at the table, she is usually too busy making sure they eat well and asking them about their day.

'Anyway, Gary was saying that as the phone becomes more important in our lives, we'll need to be more careful with it. So, he wants me to work with a team in London and the US to develop a software programme that will help the owner locate their phone if it's lost or misplaced. This will mean finding a way to activate the microphone and camera so that one can find out who has it. Even Gary doesn't know yet how to make that happen, but he was hired especially for this, so who knows? All I'm hoping for is that they'll give me a free iPhone,' Archana laughs, rather pleased with the project as well as her daughter's interest in her work.

'Wow, that sounds fascinating, Amma. You do such interesting stuff.'

'Yeah, yeah. What do you want, Sini, that you are buttering her up?' Raju slides a little more rice and curd onto his plate and continues, 'But seriously, your mother is the smartest person I know. Note I said person, not woman.'

'Oh, Raju. Now what do YOU want from me?'

The banter gets them all into a good mood and the stress of the last exam is forgotten for a brief while. After dinner, Shalu goes back to her room while Raju and Archana clear the table. Then Raju sits down with his laptop to check how his investments are doing in the choppy markets.

'I have a short presentation to write,' Archana tells him as she leaves the room. 'Won't be more than half an hour.'

'I hope I am still awake then.'

In a few hours the house settles into the calm silence of a household at peace, with only the ticking of the old Ajanta wall clock to be heard.

## 3

Archana is up early the next day to bathe and pray for Shalu, while Raju sets off on his morning walk around the apartment complex. Shalu herself is still waking up, willing the morning to get over quickly. She is looking forward to a few days of fun with her friends before the entrance exams for the various engineering colleges take up all their time, IIT being on top of everyone's list.

A couple of hours later, it's time to leave.

Raju stands in the doorway, looking dapper in a navy blue shirt and beige trousers. Car keys in hand, he calls out to Shalu, 'Sini baby, I'm ready. Let's leave before the traffic builds up. I'll drop you to the exam centre one last time.'

'Who are you calling baby, Appa? I'm seventeen years old,' says Shalu in mock anger. Hands on her hips, dressed in her school uniform of navy blue trousers and dark blue jacket over a white shirt, she tosses her hair back like a model facing a camera.

'Oh, you can be fifty-seven but you'll still be my baby,' Raju says, laughing at his daughter's antics.

'Bye, Amma. Wish me luck.' Shalu walks up to Archana, who hugs her, then puts a dot of vibhuti on her forehead.

'Always, chinnu. My blessings are always with you. I know you have studied very hard and I am sure you can answer every question in the exam and top your school. Remember what I said, answer the easy questions first so that you have time for the more difficult ones. Revise everything before handing over the papers. And now come here, have some prasad for God's blessings as well. I just made it.'

'Thanks, Amma.' Shalu rolls her eyes at this religious intervention. 'See you in the evening.'

'Is there anything you want me to buy for the dinner with Prasad and Janet? I can easily hop into Fatima's next door during lunch,' Raju says.

'I thought we'd keep it simple. Maybe some Kozhi gassi, bisi bele and dahi bada. We can order in neer dosa to go with that. And dessert. Prasad loves the cham chams from KC Das.'

Shalu and Raju head out, leaving the house to Archana for the next thirty minutes. She brews a cup of coffee and then reads the morning papers, sitting in the balcony and occasionally looking out at the trees in the park, trying to catch a glimpse of a bulbul or the noisy parakeets that nest there.

Meanwhile, Raju fights his way through the morning traffic, shaking his head at the drivers who blatantly disregard lanes and rules.

'One day I'm going to lose it completely and shoot someone,' he grumbles.

'Oh, Appa, nothing's going to change, ever. Don't let it spoil your mood,' says Shalu, moving closer and putting her head on his shoulder, as she does whenever she wants to distract him. 'Let's talk about something fun. Looking forward to the evening with Prasad Uncle and Aunty Janet?'

'Oh yes, Sini, you know I always enjoy their company. They have such stories to tell about their world of movies and magic. You remember, the last time we met, they were talking about this top film star who walked out of a shoot because he didn't like some dish on the menu. He only came back when the caterer was fired and a whole new menu was made available. It's like their industry is full of big egos and crazy people.'

He turns to glance at Shalu. 'You'll be home, right, when they come?'

'Yes, I should be. I'll probably catch up with some friends afterwards and come home by 8 or 8.30 p.m. latest.'

She grins wickedly at him. 'You know I really love Aunty Janet. And not only because she usually has some little gift for me.'

Raju bursts out laughing, then curses as an overloaded tractor carrying rubble suddenly cuts in front of their car causing him to brake suddenly. The car behind him honks in anger. But the driver of the tractor is too busy chatting with someone beside him to realise he has nearly caused an accident. Raju overtakes the lumbering vehicle with another blast of the horn to merge with the traffic turning towards the school.

Around the time that father and daughter drive into the exam centre, Archana grabs her helmet and rides off to her office. It's only fifteen minutes away, but last night's rain will make it a bit longer.

4

Saturday morning is temple time. Raju and Archana visit the Ganesha temple that is only a few minutes' drive away. Shalu is sleeping in. They do their puja and on the way back, on an impulse, Raju stops at an Udupi restaurant to get coffee for both of them. Raju is not one for grand gestures or showing his feelings openly. But he makes up with these little impulsive moves that surprise Archana and underline the depth of his affection for her.

It's close to nine by the time they get home. Archana rustles up some dosas for them and for a still sleepy Shalini, then everyone gets busy tidying up the house in preparation for the evening. Raju puts away the unread newspapers and sets up the bar, Shalini lays the table, while Archana arranges the flowers in the living room.

As soon as the work is done, Shalu retires to her room to get ready for her afternoon out. She is to meet her friends at their favourite hangout, a club called Malibu, off Brigade Road. On weekends, the club opens at 2 p.m. with a DJ belting out loud dance music, including the latest hits in English, Hindi, Kannada and Tamil, through extra-large, extra-loud speakers. The cheap soft drinks and food act as a magnet for the city's youth, who yearn for a place where they can act adult. At sharp 6 p.m., the DJ winds up his act and so do the teenagers. By seven, the bar lights are on, the music gets softer, and two bartenders turn up to get things ready for the older clientele who will soon arrive. But between two and six, the place is perfectly safe, and fun, for young people, so Raju and Archana have no qualms about Shalu heading there.

'Amma, I am leaving.'

'Wait, wait. Let me look at you once before you rush out,' Archana says. Shalu laughs and pirouettes for her, showing off the new skirt Janet got her for Christmas, which she hasn't had a chance to wear before. It's dark blue with tiny silver stars embroidered on. A fawn-coloured, big-collared blouse and a pair of silver strap high heels complete the look.

'Oh, you look gorgeous, my rani. Look after yourself. Remember to …'

'One, stay with your friends. Two, don't accept food or drinks from anyone else. Three, don't be too late. Four, call if you need Appa to come and pick you up,' Shalini interrupts, ticking the list off on her fingers. 'How many times are you going to say the same things? I'm all grown up now. I can take care of myself,' she grumbles.

'You can turn fifty and if I'm around then, I'll still tell you the same things.'

'Amma …' Shalu sighs in exasperation.

'Anyway, how will you come home? Want Appa to pick you up?'

Before Shalini can reply, Raju interrupts them. 'Really? Will anyone ask me before committing my time?'

'Don't worry, Appa. I'll come back with one of my friends. Maybe Tabassum. Her father will be coming to pick her up and you know they live just two streets away.'

'Ok. Anyway, I'm kidding, you know that. If you need me, just call. What time will we see you back?' Raju gives Shalini a tight hug. 'After all that studying and stress, you deserve an evening out.'

'I think, at about 8 or 8.30? After the club, we may grab a snack somewhere before heading home.'

As she leaves with a wave and a goodbye, Raju shakes his head in bemusement. 'Seventeen going on forty. She sounds so mature and confident.'

'That's true. When I was looking for something today morning I found one of her baby albums. Remember that time when we went to Brindavan Gardens? She was just about two then. All dressed up in that cute frilly skirt and a big floppy hat. You were carrying her on your shoulders so that she could see the fountains. And now look at her. I pray that Lord Ganesha always looks out for her.'

'When shall I order the neer dosas? Eight o'clock good enough?' asks Raju.

'Yes, I think so. We can serve dinner at 9 or 9.30 depending on how the evening is going. Did you put the cham chams in the fridge?'

'Yes, I did that just after we returned this morning.'

'Oh, they'll be nice and chilled by the time we have dinner. I'm sure Janet will bring something as well.' Archana empties packets of banana chips and peanuts into bowls on the centre table.

'Ok, looks like we're all set. I'll have a bath and get dressed.'

'I'll just check on Shalu,' says Raju, picking up his phone to send her a text.

*'Hello Sini. Just checking that you reached safe.'*

'*Yes Appa. Having fun,*' comes the response ten minutes later.

An hour later, the doorbell rings. The Raos have arrived.

Janet is dressed to the hilt as usual, in her favourite gold and white stilettos, white capris and a green kurti. Her hair is pulled back elegantly and she is wearing light make-up.

'Come in, come in. Janet, you look amazing as always,' says Raju as he leans forward to hug her.

'It's so nice to be able to see you guys. Feels like it's been a really long time,' she replies, returning the hug warmly.

Janet and Prasad are highly sought-after producers in the television industry. Back when they were in school with Archana, nobody would have guessed that was the direction their lives would take, given how they languished in the grades department, then and in college. But a lucky break for Janet in a small role in a successful TV show opened the doors for both of them. Their hard work coupled with a few lucky breaks brought them their first big success as producers of a game show. It was among the first on Indian TV, which was used to highly scripted and over-the-top melodrama. Its success led to a few other reality shows followed by a few hit series, and now they are among the crème de la crème of the television world with even a few leading movie stars jostling to work with them. They have no children of their own, so Shalu is fortuitously blessed with another set of parents who lavish affection on her.

'Hi, Janet,' Archana says with a big smile on her face for her old friend. 'Come, sit next to me. We have so much to catch up on. I can't even remember when we met last.' Before Janet can reply, Prasad appears in the doorway, flamboyant in linen trousers and a floral half-sleeve shirt. It has taken him some time finding parking space.

'Hello, hello! You've already started gup-shupping, have you?'

Raju grins at him. 'Prasad, I wish I could say we missed you, but I'd be lying.'

'We didn't even know you were here, Raju. Otherwise, we'd have come another day,' Prasad retorts. He looks at Archana. 'My friend. Why has it been so long since we met?'

'I think we met last for Diwali? That's six months back. Wow!'

'Oh yes. You brought that lovely mithai from Rajasthan.'

'Right, I remember Shalu had two straight from the box, immediately.' Everyone laughs at the memory.

'Speaking of Shalu, where's my darling? I have a little something just for her, from the sets of our last movie.'

'Oh, she's gone out with some friends, celebrating the end of school. But she'll be back before you go, don't worry.'

'Come, sit, Prasad, your throne awaits you,' says Archana.

'Thanks.' Prasad settles down in his favourite spot in the Gowda house. The ancient rocking chair that belonged to Archana's grandfather is still going strong.

'So, how did her exams go?' asks Janet as Raju shuts the main door and walks back into the living room.

'She said they went ok, but you can never tell. If she wants to get into one of the IITs, she'll need to do well in the entrance exams as well. I am praying every day to every god I can think of, that she gets what she wants. Finally, it's not in our hands.'

'God helps those who help themselves,' interjects Raju. 'And I think it's time we started helping ourselves. Janet, I've got a bottle of your favourite wine chilling since yesterday. Shall I pour you a glass? Or do you want something stronger?'

'Wine would be perfect, thank you. But only if Archana will join me as well.'

Archana makes a face. 'Just half a glass for me, Raju. You know I am good for nothing after one glass. I'll probably end up talking rubbish.'

'Yes, yes. We want to hear our super intelligent classmate talk rubbish,' says Prasad, nudging Raju.

'Let me get her half a glass first, then we'll see. Prasad, I assume the usual for you too?'

'Yup. Nothing's changed for the last twenty years on that front.'

'Ok. Give me two minutes.'

Raju goes to fix the drinks while Prasad steps out into the balcony to look out over the city, which is settling into night. Though the Gowdas live not too high up, on the third floor, their building is unusually situated in that there is no other structure next to it, so there's a clear and unobstructed view of the city. Right now, the night lights are gleaming as far as the eye can see.

Back in the living room, Janet turns to Archana. 'So what are Shalu's plans for the holidays?'

Before Archana can answer, her phone rings. She looks at the name lighting up the screen and gets a puzzled look on her face.

'Tabassum?' she says as she picks up the phone.

Raju is just walking in with two glasses of wine. 'Tabassum? But it's only past eight. I hope everything is ok.'

Archana puts the phone on speaker mode as she answers. 'Hello, Tabassum. Is everything ok?'

Tabassum's voice is hesitant over the phone. 'Aunty, I don't know. Can you come to Malibu, please?'

Archana's face crumples in panic. 'Why? What's happened? Is Shalu ok?'

'Aunty, can you come quickly?' Tabassum repeats.

'What's the matter? Has something happened to Shalu? Can I speak to her?'

'Aunty, I don't think Shalu wants to talk to anyone. Please come quickly.'

The phone goes dead as Tabassum hangs up and Archana turns to Raju, bewildered.

'Ok. Ok, so nothing has happened to Shalu. That's a relief. But why did Tabassum call? Why not Shalu?'

'Archana, I'll go with Raju,' says Prasad, standing up and picking up his car keys. 'It's probably just a fight among the girls.'

'A fight would be so unlikely. They haven't had one in all these years.'

She gets up and goes into her room, picks up her handbag and slips on sandals. 'I can't just sit here and wait, Prasad. I'm coming with you both. Let's all go.'

'Let me get my wallet and phone. Don't worry, Archana. It must be something minor that Tabassum panicked about. You know how anxious she gets over little things.'

'Yes, I know, but still … I need to see Shalu.'

She mutters a quick prayer under her breath. 'Oh God, I know you are looking after my family, so I leave everything in your hands. Please look after Shalu, please please please. That's all I ask.'

# 5

There is silence in the car as they drive down to Malibu, the club tucked into a side lane in the heart of the city. It's Saturday evening and the roads are busy. Prasad attempts to make small talk to lighten the mood, but gives up quickly and focuses on navigating the traffic.

They drive up to the entrance of the club and Prasad lets the others out before moving on to find a parking slot. Being a Saturday evening, this may be more challenging than usual. Seeing Archana step out of the car, Tabassum comes running up.

'Aunty, come this way.'

'What's going on, Tabassum? You're scaring me.'

'Shalu is just sitting there, Aunty, she's not saying anything. I don't know what happened, but it's scary watching her like that. That's why I called you.'

'Shalu!' Archana exclaims as she spots the slim form hunched on a bench near the edge of the parking lot, hidden from the view of those inside. Her head is down and her arms are wrapped around her middle as if she is in pain. Archana runs up and pulls her close in a tight embrace. 'I am so glad you're safe. I was so worried.'

'What happened to your face, Sini? Are those scratch marks? Is that blood?' asks Raju.

Archana pulls back and looks at Shalu properly. There are long, jagged marks on her forehead and cheeks. Streaks of blood.

'What happened, Shalu? Who did this to you? And why is your dress torn? What happened, Shalu?' Archana's voice rises in a panicked scream.

'Shalu, what's going on? Tell us!' Raju says urgently.

Shalu remains motionless, her eyes closed, her body stiff in Archana's arms. Her voice is barely audible when she speaks. 'I want to go home,' she says. 'Take me home.'

The adults gathered around her are frozen into silence. Archana feels the bile rise inside here, a dawning sense of horror and hopelessness. What has happened to her child? She wraps her arms tighter around Shalu and tries to blank out all thoughts for a moment.

Janet breaks the silence. 'Let me call Prasad and ask him to bring the car. We'll go home, Shalu,' she says gently.

Shalu looks up unseeingly, her eyes wet, tears pouring down her cheeks. She tries to stand up and stumbles.

'Shalu, what is it? Are you hurt? Please tell us!' Archana is frantic as she holds up her daughter, her own eyes spilling over with tears.

Prasad walks up to them. 'All ok?' he asks.

'I don't know. Shalu, say something! Are you in pain? Who did this to you? Why do you have these marks on your face?'

Raju turns to Tabassum, who is crying too and watching Shalu with despair written large on her face. 'What happened, Tabassum? Why is Shalu crying? What happened to her?'

Tabassum looks from Raju to Prasad, then her eyes lock on to Shalu's and she pulls away.

'I ... I ...' she stutters.

'What's going on? Why don't you say something?' asks Janet exasperatedly. 'For heaven's sake, we need to know.'

'Aunty, I don't know either. All I know is, we all came out after the music stopped. Then Thomas offered to drop Shalu home.'

'Which Thomas? Thomas Chacko? Your classmate?'

'Yes, Thomas. He was with us all evening, with some of his friends. Afterwards, he offered to drop Shalu home because my father wanted me to go meet him in his restaurant. We came out and then we found that Thomas didn't have a ride of his own. But his friend, Palani, had a car and he said your house was on his way. Then Thomas, Palani and Shalu got into the car and drove away. I still had some time before getting to the restaurant, so I went back into the club. Many of our friends were still around. When I came out again at about 8 o'clock, I saw Shalu sitting here like this.'

Archana clasps Shalini closer. 'What happened, my baby? Did anyone do anything to you? Are you hurt?' she whispers.

Shalini does not respond. Only the tears flow unchecked from her vacant eyes.

Raju's heart seems to stop as he looks at his daughter. It has been so long since he saw her cry. He is also beginning to lose patience. They have been standing around for over fifteen minutes, no wiser to the problem at hand. 'Shalu, tell us what happened. We can't keep standing here like this. People are beginning to stare at us.'

Prasad pulls Raju aside. 'You are not helping. Let's leave Janet and Archu to it.'

He takes out a pack of cigarettes and offers one to Raju.

Raju gave up smoking many years ago, but he reaches for a cigarette gratefully. Anything to calm his nerves. His mind is swirling in confusion. Something has happened to his darling. It scares him. 'What do you think Prasad?' he asks, taking a long drag before exhaling the smoke.

'Don't know, Raju. Obviously, she is in pain and looks injured. I hope it's nothing serious. Let's wait to see what Archu and Janet find out.'

The light of a swanky car driving into the parking lot flashes on Raju's grim face as he continues to puff away at his cigarette.

Suddenly, a loud, wrenching cry cuts through his thoughts. There's something wild and uncontrolled and frightening about it. The voice sounds like Archana's, but he has never heard a more chilling sound before. He is too shocked to react till Prasad shakes him, saying, 'Raju, come. Something's wrong.' They turn and rush towards the women.

Archana is wailing as she holds Shalini tight, so tight that it looks like she might suffocate her. Janet and Tabassum are holding on to each other and in tears as well.

Raju is gripped with fear.

'What happened, Archu,' he asks frantically. 'What happened?'

Archana looks at him over Shalu's head, the words refusing to form on her lips. 'Raju, Shalu … oh God, our Shalu …'

Raju struggles to respond, knowing something terrible has happened but unable to comprehend what it could be. He wraps his arms around Archana and Shalu fiercely, fighting back tears. He can hear Janet and Prasad talking in hushed murmurs. 'What! No!' Prasad says, his voice rising in anger and shock.

Raju can't hold off the realisation anymore. His Shalu, his Sini … He can't bring himself to even think of what may have happened. He has read about girls being assaulted and heard about it on TV, but it was always something that happened to other parents and their daughters.

Shalini's voice breaks through his thoughts, barely audible. 'I am sorry, Amma. I am sorry,

Appa.' Her body is trembling, she can barely stand without support.

'Don't say that, Shalu.' Archana's voice is anguished. 'How is it your fault? How can you say sorry?'

'We need to call the cops, Raju. This is serious,' says Prasad, starting to take control of the situation. Raju and Archana look at him, equally helpless. They are aware that time is of the essence. They need to act.

# 6

'Janet, I think you should take Shalu home now. Let me call Venky,' says Prasad.

Venky is Prasad's man Friday whose job it is to know people and how to get things done.

Venky picks up the phone instantly. 'What's happening, boss? How come calling on a Saturday night? Everything ok?'

'Venky, we have a problem. A friend's daughter has had an accident. Who do you know in the police who can help?' Prasad asks, walking away from the others.

'What kind of accident, boss? Normal traffic accident, just go to …'

'No, not a traffic accident. Something to do with a … a girl kind of accident.'

'Oh, I am sorry, boss. When it comes to that kind of thing, the police are very strict. There are guidelines from above and everyone has to follow it, or they can lose their jobs. So, first, have to call 1908. Within minutes, the police will arrive and then the system will take over. Once the basic work is done, the case will be assigned to a police inspector. Then we can use our connections and see what best can be done. So boss, call 1908 right now. Where are you? I'll come there.'

'No, no need for you to come, Venky. If there's anything, I'll call you later. Let me call 1908 and see what happens. But be on standby, ok?'

'Boss, is it serious? Anyone I know?'

'Yes, it is very serious. But it's not anybody you know. Good friends of ours. Ok, let me go now. Will call you back.'

Just as he is dialling the number Venky has given him, he hears Raju approaching. 'Did you find out what is to be done? Who should we call?'

'Don't worry, Raju. I'll call every single person I know. But first let me call the police. I am told there is a process in place to tackle such matters.'

'Hello, police?'

In a few minutes there is a police jeep and an ambulance in the car park. Tabassum replays what she told Archana and Raju a few minutes earlier. A policewoman talks to Shalini for a few minutes, then tells her that she will need to come to the hospital for a medical check-up. Archana and Janet can go along too.

A policeman in uniform, probably in his late thirties, walks up to Raju and Prasad. 'I'm Sub-inspector Varma with the Bangalore Metro Police. I need you to come with me to the Commercial Street station, to complete the formalities,' he says.

'I'll come with you,' Raju says. He is angry, tearful, unable to think straight. But he knows one thing. 'I want to make sure the monster who did this to Shalu goes to jail. I could kill him,' he says through clenched teeth, his fingers curled into fists.

'Absolutely, sir. That's what we want to do as well. Find the person who did it and make sure he gets the punishment he deserves. But for that we need to follow the right process, get all the facts in place. The station is less than five minutes away,' says SI Varma. 'You can follow my jeep.'

'Sub-inspector Varma, you must assure me that you'll get him, that justice will be done.'

'It will if we all do our part correctly,' replies Varma as he gets into his jeep.

'Come, let's go,' says Prasad, putting an arm around Raju and leading him to his car.

A few minutes later, they are at the Commercial Street police station where they are directed to a cabin at the end of a short corridor. SI Varma is waiting for them. He gestures for them to take the two chairs across from him. A glass of water is placed in front of each of them.

'So, this is what we'll do, ok?' he begins. 'You tell me everything that happened. I may ask you some questions till I've got everything I need. Then we'll put it all down in a First Information Report and start our investigation. What happened, where it happened, who was involved, why it happened and so on. This will form the basis for us to file a chargesheet and make a case for the Public Prosecutor. I have to warn you that these things take time, even if it all seems very obvious and straightforward to you.'

'Well, it is simple and straightforward,' says Raju. 'We have to get Thomas and some guy called Palani, who gave Shalu a lift.'

'That's good,' says SI Varma reassuringly. 'But let's start at the beginning.'

For the next hour or so, Raju and Prasad tell SI Varma all they know about what happened that evening. They give him the information he asks for, about Shalu's friends, teachers, school, and anything else that seems even remotely relevant. Finally, the sub-inspector sits back, satisfied. 'I think we can stop here. We have everything we need. You should go to your daughter. She should be home by now. You can be sure we'll go after the culprits, and get them too.'

SI Varma's sincerity and determination are evident in every word he speaks. Or so Raju would like to believe.

7

A few hours later, Raju's phone rings. It's SI Varma.

'I know it's past midnight, but can I come over? It's important,' he says.

'Of course.' Raju hangs up and turns to Prasad. Janet and Archana are inside with Shalu.

'Do you think they've got something already and he wants to update us? This could mean real progress.'

'I hope so, man. I really hope so.'

Raju pours himself a glass of water and paces the living room. Prasad, usually so full of energy and laughter, has been struck silent. He stands staring out into the dark night.

Thirty minutes have passed by the time they hear footsteps on the landing. Raju opens the door to SI Varma before he can ring the bell. The two men look at each other silently before Raju gestures an invitation into the house.

The SI steps in and pauses on seeing Prasad. He nods at him and remains standing, looking a little uncomfortable.

'Please sit,' says Prasad.

'Yes, please do sit. Can I get you anything?' Raju asks.

'No, nothing. I am ok. How is your daughter? And Madam?'

'I cannot say, Inspector Varma. So much has happened and none of us knows what lies ahead. But why did you say you want to talk to me?'

'And feel free to talk in front of Prasad,' he adds. 'He is my dearest friend. Shalini's godfather. Loves her as much as I do, maybe even more.'

The policeman relaxes. 'Well, we've done some preliminary investigation. It's not official and it's not in the records yet, but it could be in the news tomorrow.'

'In the news?' Raju can't believe his ears.

'Bloody ridiculous!' says Prasad 'Doesn't anyone have any concern for the poor child?'

'Sir, it's not like that. Your daughter's name will not be mentioned. It's illegal to mention a minor's name. Even our records on that are kept confidential. But Malibu is a high-profile club.

My men were there earlier. People talk. Then the media picks it up and spins a story. It doesn't have to be accurate, but it's still a story. That's what they're after. We can't control that.' He has the look of a man who doesn't like it but is not going to fight it.

'Someone from the women's division has already spoken to your daughter in the hospital. We'll have a follow-up meeting in the morning. From our preliminary investigations it appears that your daughter was given a lift by this boy called Palani. Thomas also went along. Along the way, they picked up two of Palani's friends. Two brothers. Ahmed and Samir. An hour later, they all returned and dropped your daughter off at the car park.'

'Four boys?' Prasad can't mask his shock. Raju is too stunned to say anything.

'Sir. There were four boys in the car, but it appears that one of them, Thomas, was not involved in the actual … incident. He was a sort of lookout.'

'Thomas?' Raju asks through his daze. 'But Thomas is a really good friend of Shalu's. He was here yesterday with Tabassum and some others.'

'Maybe that's why he did nothing, sir. We don't know. Ahmed and Samir's father runs a fairly successful real-estate business in the city. These two boys and Palani study in the same college and are in the same class. They are a troublemaking pair. Small-time stuff—eve-teasing, bullying, rash driving and so on. Nothing like this.'

He hesitates. 'Palani is the tricky one, sir.'

'Tricky? Why tricky? We know he gave her a lift. She'll identify him,' says Prasad.

'Yes, sir, and usually that would be enough. But Palani is the son of the local MLA, Mr Nanjundaswamy. We are already hearing news of meetings with lawyers. We've confiscated the car but politicians can make things happen, sir, as you know. The police department and I will do all the necessary work to put this case together. I just wanted to let you know, unofficially, that this is no longer such a simple or straightforward case.'

'Are you saying they'll get away with it? The police will stop investigating?'

'No, sir. I'm not saying anything of the sort. I'm merely stating that there are VIPs involved and that is bound to complicate matters. Anyway, I came here mostly to warn you that some news media or the other will carry this news tomorrow. But I am quite sure neither your daughter's name nor yours will come up.'

He gets up to leave. 'I'll try to keep you informed, unofficially of course. Also, please expect a call from our women's wing for the follow-up interview with your daughter. And sir, I'd advise that you get some rest. The next few days are going to be difficult.'

8

*Teenager raped in posh club. MLA's son suspected.*

Raju is the first to see the headlines in the *Deccan Herald*. Prasad comes up behind him, scrolling down on his phone to see if something has appeared in the national media. Not yet.

No one has slept in the Gowda household. Shalu is in her room, lying in bed and staring blankly at the ceiling. Janet is curled up on the armchair near the bed, dozing. Archana has cried herself into silence and has been at her prayers since dawn. The incense from the puja spreads an uneasy fragrance through the house.

Prasad and Janet decide to head home to clean up and return with breakfast for all of them. Nobody feels like cooking, but eat they must.

Suddenly, the doorbell rings. It is just 7 a.m. Unusually early for someone to come by. Archana is still in the midst of her morning prayers, her voice impassioned as she speaks to her gods.

Raju puts on his shirt as he goes to open the door.

A stranger is standing outside. Over six feet in height, swarthy complexion, crew-cut hair. Dressed in a casual blue T-shirt and khakis. There is an air of authority about him.

'Yes?'

'Mr Gowda, I am DGP Bhaskar. Can I come in?'

Oh, of course. No wonder his face looks so familiar. Raju has seen him often enough on TV, and on social media too. What is he doing here, he wonders.

'Please come in, DGP sir. Sorry, we were not expecting anyone, so the room is a bit of a mess,' Raju says distractedly as he points him to a chair. 'Can I get you some tea or coffee? Or a glass of water?'

'Oh no, nothing at all,' says DGP Bhaskar, shaking his head. 'How is Shalini?' he asks, looking around.

'She is in her room. Been locked in there since … since that happened. Doesn't talk much. Spends her time lying down or looking out of the window.'

The policeman puts a hand on Raju's shoulder. 'It's a horrible thing to have happened, Mr Gowda. I have a daughter who is only a few years older than Shalini. She's had her share of troubles with eve teasing and bullying. Nothing close to what happened to Shalini. But I understand a little bit, a father's pain …'

Raju leans forward in his chair, shrugging off the man's hand. 'I hope the guilty are punished. They should not be allowed to escape, whatever the legal loopholes they invent. You have to get us justice, DGP Bhaskar. You have to!'

'Actually, can I get a glass of water now, Mr Gowda? Room temperature is fine.' DGP Bhaskar stands up and walks to the window to look out at the small park just across the road.

Then he turns to Raju and asks, 'What do you mean by justice, Mr Gowda? What do you mean when you say you want justice?'

Raju is taken aback by the question. 'Why, the answer is obvious. Those boys who did this to Shalu must be punished, of course.'

'Is that justice? Will putting a person in jail for ten or fifteen years, or whatever the term is, be justice?'

He accepts the glass of water that Raju has brought him and walks back to his chair.

Raju watches him warily. 'Of course that is justice. When the person who commits a crime pays for it, justice is done. Your question surprises me. Why are you asking this? You are a policeman. Surely you know when justice is done?'

DGP Bhaskar smiles. 'You see, Mr Gowda, in my years in the service I have found that the term "justice" is interpreted differently by different people. Some people want the other side to be punished. Some people want the victim to be acknowledged. Some people want both. Some are philosophical and say, let God decide. That's why I asked you, what is your definition of justice?'

'DGP sir, I am very clear. The boys involved in this must be punished to the fullest extent of the law. That's it. Very simple. I hope that you are focused on the same objective.' Raju is struggling to keep his voice down. He is mindful that he doesn't want to disturb Archana's puja nor alert Shalini.

'Let me assure you, Mr Gowda, my team is diligently collecting all the information they need. SI Varma is one of the best officers we have in the force. They will do a thorough investigation so that the prosecutor has a case to file. But I wanted to talk to you in person anyway.' DGP Bhaskar sits back and crosses one leg over the other.

'Mr Gowda, I have another question for you,' he says with a curious smile on his face. 'You want justice to be done. But what price are you willing to pay for it?'

'Price? What price? These men committed a crime. The state is prosecuting them. Why do I have to pay a price?'

'Ah, you see, Mr Gowda, there is a price. All justice comes with a price,' DGP Bhaskar says matter-of-factly.

'I don't understand. Are you saying I need to bribe someone to get things moving?'

'No, no. No bribe. I'm not talking about money. Can we talk plainly, Mr Gowda?'

'I thought that's what we are doing!'

'Your daughter has accused three boys of this crime.'

'Rape. It's rape. Crime makes it sound impersonal.' Raju can hardly believe he is having an argument about the vocabulary of the violence his daughter has been subjected to, but it's important to get the facts right.

'Ok, rape. Three boys have been accused. In these past few hours, you can be sure their families have engaged the best lawyers in the city to defend them. And they will do everything they can to get them off scot-free.'

'They can do what they want. Shalini will identify them and they will go to jail.'

'Mr Gowda, it's not that simple. Are you sure she will identify the boys? Will she be willing and able to stand up in court and face these men in a room full of lawyers?'

'Yes, she will. Why won't she?'

'Have you spoken to her about it?'

'Why do I need to speak to her about it? She knows what happened to her. She told us, and your people, who did it to her.'

'Yes, I know, Mr Gowda, but facing them again will be a very emotional experience for her. Is she up to it? Do *you* think she is up to it? You told SI Varma that Shalini is a quiet person with a small group of friends. How will she face these boys in public after what they did to her? Will she even be willing to dress up and come to court? And you know, of course, that the lawyers will try to prove that it was she who led the boys on.'

'What nonsense!' Raju is so angry he can barely speak.

'Don't get me wrong. I am not saying she did. That's what the lawyers will say. They will claim she danced with Palani in the club. And that she left with him willingly. They will deliberately misinterpret something she said or did. All this time, Shalini will be there in court and will have to answer these questions. About things that she is trying to forget or things that did not happen at all.'

'But …'

DGP Bhaskar puts out a hand to stop him. 'I can expect that sometime soon, Shalini's name will appear in the newspapers.'

Raju cannot control himself any longer. 'But that is not legally permitted. They cannot do that.'

'I know,' the DGP responds calmly. 'I know, but when it comes to one's child, people will play dirty to get what they want. Imagine what will happen when Shalini's name comes out in the newspapers.'

'She will be destroyed.' Raju puts his head in his hands and collapses on the sofa.

'You see, that's exactly why I asked you, what is the price you are willing to pay, Mr Gowda? Justice can be done. Justice will be done. But there will be a price. And it will have to be paid by an innocent seventeen-year-old girl. Your daughter. Are you willing to let her pay it?

'Mr Gowda, you are not the first parent I have seen who has a simple view of how the justice system works. To an outsider, it seems very straightforward. Someone did something wrong. The police know who it is. They catch him, or her, and send them to jail. And everything becomes all right. But real life is never like that. There is an enemy who will fight tooth and nail. Will use all the tricks possible to destroy the person attacking their family. They don't care about the price they have to pay or the price you will have to pay.'

'So, what are you saying?' Raju asks, feeling deflated.

'I am not saying anything, Mr Gowda. The decision is yours. It's always yours. I just want you to be aware of what the next few days and weeks will be like for you and your family. I want you to discuss this with your family, to be prepared. Our investigations are ongoing and are independent of your decision.'

'I am really confused, DGP sir. I want the boys who attacked Shalini to pay the price for it. I am willing to do anything to make that happen. But it's not acceptable to me that Shalini should suffer any more than she already has.'

DGP Bhaskar heads for the door. Before leaving, he stops to shake Raju's hand and put a brotherly arm around him. Raju smiles uncertainly at him, then shuts the door and sinks into the sofa. What is he to do? What is he to think?

## 9

'Who was that?' asks Archana as she walks into the room.

'I'll tell you once Prasad gets here,' Raju replies. 'Let's discuss it then, so I don't have to repeat myself. I am just so weary, Archu. I don't know what to think.'

'Shall I make us some tea while we wait? Shalu is sleeping. I looked in on her a few minutes ago.'

She comes up to Raju and takes his hands in hers. 'There's no point worrying too much, Raju. God looks after his children. He will look after us as well. Let's leave it in his hands.'

Raju forces himself to meet her eyes and smile. 'Well, I hope he really comes through for us now, when we need him the most.'

Archana smiles back at him sadly and goes into the kitchen.

They have just finished their tea when the doorbell rings, announcing Prasad's arrival.

Prasad declines Archana's offer of tea and settles down to listen. In a few brief sentences, Raju relates the gist of his conversation with DGP Bhaskar. By the time he finishes, Archana's eyes have welled up and she is struggling to keep calm.

Prasad shakes his head in disbelief. 'This is bullshit. I can't believe it. Did the DGP just come and tell you why you should not proceed with the case?'

'Well, not exactly, Prasad. He was telling me what to expect. I actually think he was being helpful, warning us about what lies ahead. I would not have thought of these things at all, just blundered on blindly.'

'Yes, true, but what does he want us to do? Sit quietly and pretend nothing has happened? How is that justice? What happens to Shalu? I understand that he came as a friend, but a real friend would have told you how to navigate this. Not warn you about what will happens if you proceed down this path. Let me talk to Salve and find out what his legal brain makes of all this.'

'What are you thinking, Archana?' asks Raju.

'I am confused. I know I don't want Shalu's name mentioned in the newspapers. She is already so vulnerable. I don't want to make her even more miserable than she is. That is my only focus. I don't even want to think this, but maybe the DGP is right. Maybe we should let God deal with these criminals, not push things too much.'

'Archana, those boys assaulted Shalini. How can we just let them go?'

'I am not saying they should not be punished. I want to see them suffer, and badly. But I want to keep my daughter away from the media and the mess even more.' Archana gets up shakily, her voice trembling as she adds, 'I can't think about this anymore. Whatever will be, will be. Let's hear what Salve has to say and then decide.'

Prasad arranges to speak to his lawyer later that day to get a dispassionate perspective on the matter. This whole situation is new to him as well and while justice needs to be done, the impact on Shalini needs to be considered. Salve is an old friend of Prasad's and has been his go-to person for anything to do with the law. He also has friends in high places, including among the cops. If anyone knows what needs to be done, it will be Salve.

Unfortunately, Salve is not very upbeat. 'Yes, everything you are saying is right, Prasad. The law exists and it must take its course. But this is India. There will be leaks. Media stories will appear, especially given who is involved. You need to be patient and have enormous strength to see this through to the end. I am not even talking about the money required to fight the case. This girl will be ruined, and her family too. She will not be able to go to college or travel—she won't even be able to step outside her house for a while. I don't know this DGP Bhaskar too well. It may well be that he is a decent fellow, but he would not be above some politics himself and I am sure he knows which side his bread is buttered. As your friend, let me tell you, I have no problem taking this case on at all. It's a good fight to get into. But remember, I won't be the one paying the price. Nor will you. That will be for a seventeen-year-old girl to do.'

'So, what do we bloody do, Salve? Doing nothing is not an option, no?'

'You are not going to like what I tell you, but it may be the best option in this situation. Try to get something out of it. Justice is a big word, and we know how hard it is. But is there something else you can go after the criminals' families with? Is there anything the victim's families need? Tell the other party you are willing to withdraw the complaint if you get something in return. Money is the most obvious and common ask. Use the DGP as the go-between to approach them. As far as I know, this Palani fellow comes from a very wealthy family. Anyway, his father is a politician, so cash is not a problem. Samir and Ahmed are not badly off either. Between them they can put together some money for sure.'

'How the hell can you put money …' Prasad splutters, unable to complete the sentence.

Salve interrupts him. 'I told you, you won't like it, but this may be your only option. Of course, they could just let it all go and quietly move to another town and restart life there. My dispassionate recommendation is to at least get something out of it. But if you decide you want to fight the case, I am with you all the way. After all, I am a parent too. I live in this city. I don't want these fellows to go scot-free.'

'I find this whole thing absurd. We have an innocent victim. A seventeen-year-old girl whose life has been destroyed. We know who did it. Yet it seems that nothing will happen to them unless the victim is willing to pay an even bigger price. Does that sound like justice to you, Salve? Does it?'

'Who says the world is a fair place, Prasad? That's only in fairy tales, or in the movies. In the real world, the person with the connections, with the money, gets things done their way. Everyone else pays the price.'

'Salve, what the hell do I tell the parents?'

'You are the movie man. I'm sure you'll think of something. Work the facts into a believable story. Get them to understand that they don't really have an option. Quite frankly, nothing will happen to the boys.' Salve breaks off, then says, 'Listen, I have a flight to catch. Call me for anything at all. I'm telling you again, if you want to fight this case, I'll be at your side. I'll even do it pro bono. But the enemy is formidable and has no ethics, remember that.'

Prasad disconnects the call, wondering what to tell Raju and Archana, and how. He feels exhausted, emotionally drained. Besides, he has neglected work these last few days. He needs to at least arrange things so that others can keep the office functioning in his absence. He has no idea how long this will take, but he knows he needs to be there for the Gowdas.

Janet is already home. They look at each other wordlessly as she opens the door for him. He pours them each a Johnnie Walker, neat, and sits in the balcony looking at the shimmering lights of the city. Wondering what else is happening out there, in the dark underground, that will be swept away in the clear light of day.

## 10

A few kilometres away, the Gowdas are finishing an early dinner. Janet dropped off a hamper of food earlier in the day, and Shalini has actually come out of her room to eat half a sandwich. Not much is said; the air is heavy with an unspoken grief.

The doorbell rings.

Raju and Archana look at each other warily. Who could it be, so late? Unless Prasad and Janet are back.

Raju opens the door to find a stranger with his finger still hovering by the doorbell. A smallish man with a heavy moustache, short black hair parted in the middle and combed back. He is carrying a suitcase.

'Mr Gowda. Myself Ajay from MLA Nanjundaswamy. Can I come inside? We have something important to talk about.'

'Nanjundaswamy?' Raju is puzzled. Who is this? And why is someone from the MLA's office here to see him? He turns to look at Archana, to see if she is any wiser. By the look in her eyes, it seems she is.

'Palani's father,' she says softly.

Then the penny drops, and Raju remembers that MLA Nanjundaswamy is the father of one of the boys who attacked Shalu.

'Nanjundaswamy? Where is he hiding his son? And how dare you come to our house? We have nothing to say to you!' He moves to slam the door shut.

'DGP Prasad came here today, no?'

Raju is stunned. How does this fellow know about the DGP's visit?

'We know everything, Mr Gowda,' Ajay says. 'Let me come in and we can talk without the neighbours hearing. Then I'll leave.'

Reluctantly Raju opens the door wider and allows Ajay to enter.

'I won't take long,' the MLA's man says matter-of-factly. 'MLA has an offer for you. Ten crores to withdraw the complaint. Five crores are here right now in this suitcase. Five crores when the complaint is withdrawn. With this money you can move to another city, maybe another country. Your daughter's college education anywhere in the world will be taken care of. Many things can be done with this amount of money. You can move on. Otherwise, as the DGP says, her life and your entire family's life will become hell. You have to make the choice. And you have to do it by tomorrow.'

'How dare you come to our house and threaten us? You think you can get away with this? And the DGP is part of it too? Wait till the newspapers read about this!'

'Sir, no use being emotional right now. You have to think about the options in front of you. Newspapers will not print anything against the MLA. They are afraid of him and the party. They depend on us for their existence, you see. So no one else is involved in this. It's just you and us. Take the money, drop the case and lead your life. Or reject the money and live in fear forever.'

'Do you have any children, Ajay?' Archana asks softly.

'Madam, it does not matter what I have or feel or think. At the end of the day, what matters is what are the real choices you have and what you want to do about it. Think sensibly, not emotionally. We make many mistakes when we use our heart. The head usually keeps us safe.'

Suddenly Shalu appears in front of them, a pale wraith of a figure, her body trembling with suppressed rage.

'How dare you!' She lunges at Ajay and Raju has to step in between them to prevent her from hitting the man. 'Your MLA can keep his money. His son is a criminal, a monster, and he must pay the price for what he did to me. No amount of money is going to keep me quiet. Get out. Now!'

She goes to the main door, opens it and gestures to Ajay to leave.

Ajay looks at Raju and Archana, stands up, then says firmly, 'Think about what I said and let the DGP know.'

'Take your suitcase with you,' Shalini hisses angrily, pointing at the offending object.

'I'll pick it up in the morning,' Ajay says nonchalantly as he walks to the lift.

Shalini shuts the door and leans back against it, exhausted after the sudden burst of energy. 'How dare they offer us money? Who do they think we are? I am surprised you didn't say anything. And who is this DGP? What did he say?' She is so angry, there are tears running down her cheeks.

Archana looks at her beseechingly. 'Come here, my magu. Come and sit here. There are many things for us to think about. Let Appa and I talk.'

'What's there to talk about? They want to give us a lot of money to keep our mouths shut.'

'That's exactly it. It's a lot of money. And we need to be sure that if we don't shut our mouths, justice will be done.'

'My God. I can't believe you are actually thinking of keeping the money. My parents? Their only daughter has been raped by three boys, and they are thinking of making money from it. I can't take this anymore.' She looks at them with undisguised contempt before stumbling back into her room and shutting the door behind her.

Raju and Archana look at each other, grief written large on their faces. It's clear to them now that the DGP is also part of the conspiracy. All that sympathetic talk about 'I am a father too' was an act. And, truly, the media will bend the way the wind blows.

It's Archana who breaks the silence. 'Let's go to bed, Raju. It's been a long day for everyone. Let's talk about it in the morning with Shalu and then we'll do what she says. So far we have protected her from the world. But if she says she is not scared, then we should stand beside her. I know she is young, but let's tell her all that we know and then decide.'

She gets up and switches off the lights. Hopefully, tomorrow will bring them some answers.

## 11

Shalini is still stewing over Ajay's arrogant assumption that a suitcase full of money is enough to buy their silence. How can her parents even contemplate keeping the money? Surely their daughter's happiness should matter more than any amount of cash? And who is this DGP and what did he say to them? There is no question about who is right and who is wrong in the case. She is the wronged one and the right thing for everyone to do is to ensure that the three boys go to jail for what they have done to her. Are her parents so weak?

A few hours later, still unable to sleep, Shalini decides to go down to the ground-floor play area. Maybe a walk will clear her head. She opens the door and takes the three flights of stairs to the garden, slowly, painfully. There is nobody else there, all is dark and quiet. She lowers herself carefully on to a deck chair. Her body feels like a mass of jangling nerve ends and it hurts to even sit down, despite the painkillers they've pumped into her. She looks at her hands, at her jagged nails and bruised knuckles, and her fists close in remembered pain and fury. Their bodies rushing at her, the hands clasping her mouth shut, her clothes ripping, the twisting, turning agony of trying to escape, to push their weight away, to hit out at the faces hovering over hers. She squeezes her eyes shut and tries to fight the rising panic, block the memories out. Gradually, her breathing returns to normal and she lies back, forcing her body to stretch out and relax. The night sky is bright with stars and she focuses on them, seeking out the constellations and naming each one aloud with some effort. Before she knows it, sleep has overtaken her.

She wakes up with a start, loud voices breaking through the fog of sleep. She can see it's morning already.

She walks slowly to the side of the building, careful to keep out of sight in case there are people nearby. It takes her a few moments to register the sight that meets her eyes. Her mother, surrounded by policemen, being half led and half dragged by two women, also in police uniform, towards a police jeep that is waiting with its engine running. She can hear her crying and calling her name. Shrieks of 'Shalu, Shalu'. That must be what woke her. Just as she is about to step out, a stretcher is wheeled out into the driveway. On it lies a body, encased in what looks like a body bag. Then a police car draws up and she hears someone call out, 'DGP sir, here.'

She watches as the uniformed policeman walks to the stretcher and unzips the body bag. Her own body spasms in shock as she recognises the shape of her father.

The DGP seems to be asking one of the other officers something. The man shakes his head. There are people milling about everywhere and then she sees something that turns her blood cold. Just beside the last police jeep is the man who had come last night with the money. Ajay. He is standing there quietly watching the action. At one point, the DGP and he exchange glances and the policeman shrugs his shoulders before turning his eyes back to the body on the stretcher. Ajay nods and melts away.

Shalini does not understand what is going on, but she knows it could be dangerous for her. She could be in deep trouble if she is found. She backs into the park, climbs over the low wall with some difficulty, and walks as fast as she can, away from her home.

## 12

### Bribery Attempt Leads to Murder

Yesterday, a gruesome tragedy occurred in a peaceful neighbourhood of South Bangalore. Rajesh Gowda, a respected finance manager at a prominent cement supplier, was brutally slain by his very own wife as he slept.

It has been revealed that tensions between the couple had been high due to money issues and a suitcase filled with 2 crore rupees in cash was discovered on the premises.

Briefing the press, DGP Bhaskar divulged further details of the family's troubled past. It appears that the Gowdas' daughter had recently accused MLA Nanjundaswamy's son of rape. The parents had demanded 5 crore rupees from Nanjundaswamy to withdraw the charge. In an attempt to protect his son's reputation, he complied and sent an assistant with part of the money, with promises of the remaining amount being given once the case was dropped. Later that night, it is thought that Mr and Mrs Gowda got into an argument which ended with her plunging a knife into her husband's abdomen no fewer than 27 times, killing him almost instantly.

When the police arrived after calls from neighbours who were alarmed by the strange noises coming from the apartment, Mrs Gowda was found attempting to clean a bloody knife in the kitchen sink. She has since been arrested. Their daughter is unaccounted for. However, there is no indication that she was involved in the scheme to blackmail Nanjundaswamy.

## 13

SI Varma cannot believe what he is reading. It is so obviously and blatantly wrong. He runs up the two flights of stairs to DGP Bhaskar's room.

He salutes his superior and starts, 'Good morning, sir. I saw the news report on the Nanjundaswamy case. I think we are mistaken, sir. I met the girl, sir, that night. I am sure everything happened the way we first documented it.'

'Varma, hold on,' interrupts the senior officer, an annoyed look on his face. 'Are you saying what I said is wrong?'

'Well, sir, maybe it is.'

'Maybe what? Listen to me, Varma. I like you and I believe you have a great future in the department. You may even become DGP one day. But you need to understand that some things are best left alone. This is one of those. People have intervened and things have been decided.'

'But sir …'

'Don't interrupt me, Varma. This is done. We'll close the case and move on. I don't want to hear about it anymore. You can leave now.'

Varma is stunned. He has never been spoken to like this by the DGP. As he is walking back to his desk, his phone rings. It is Prasad. Again.

There have been several missed calls since the morning, all of which Varma has ignored as he has no information to share.

'Hello, Mr Prasad.'

'Don't you hello me, you bastard!' Prasad's voice explodes over the phone. 'What is this bullshit I am reading? Everything is made up, is it? You know the rape happened. You know who did it. Why is your boss spouting these lies? You really think Archana is capable of murder? Fucking liars, that's what you are. I'm coming to see you now.'

'Wait, sir. Don't come here. I'll meet you elsewhere. At the coffee shop in the Lifestyle mall off MG road. In half an hour.'

'Why? Why not at the police station?'

'See you in half an hour and then we'll talk,' Varma replies.

Unknown to him, transfer orders out of the state are already being readied for him. Moving Varma to some place far away will keep him out of the hair of the local authorities. He won't be a nuisance to anyone else nor will he harm his own career attempting anything foolhardy. And that, DGP Bhaskar has decided, would be best for all of them.

A half hour later, Prasad walks into the coffee shop and is beckoned to a corner table by Varma.

'What the hell is this, Varma? What is going on? So much in one day? The case has been changed, my friend is dead, his wife has been arrested. And no one knows anything about Shalini.' Prasad is furious, but also despairing.

'Sir, I don't know what to say. This is the first time I've been involved in something of this sort. It's being done at the highest level. MLA Nanjundaswamy is very influential and a potential CM candidate. He is doing everything possible to get out of this cleanly. Doesn't want any shadow to hang over him, I suppose. I spoke to the DGP, but he is hand in glove with the man. I also made a few calls and everyone said the same thing. They'll bury the case and make it about the Gowdas.'

Varma pauses as a waiter comes up to ask if they would like to order something. Prasad waves him away impatiently.

'With one person dead and Mrs Gowda not saying anything, there's no one to speak for Shalini,' Varma continues. 'She herself is missing since the night before. We are searching for her, but so far, no confirmed location. Someone said she was seen near the bus stand yesterday morning, but after that, not a trace of her.'

'Do you really think that Archana killed Raju? She's one of the softest, gentlest people I've ever met. I've known her for more than thirty years. I don't think I've even seen her get angry, not once. And now she's being made out to be some kind of witch who murdered her own husband.'

Prasad takes a deep breath and looks Varma in the eye, trying to find the words to explain to him how absurd and outrageous the very thought is. 'They were so much in love with each other, and so intensely protective of Shalu. I don't know where that money came from, but it was never an issue with them. Obviously, this is all part of a conspiracy.'

'Sir, from the information we have, it seems that some people came to their house late in the night. The door was open for some reason, but it would not have mattered anyway. They would have got in somehow.' Varma is whispering now. 'They chloroformed Mrs Gowda before stabbing her husband to death. Then they planted the knife in her hand. About two or three hours later, they placed an anonymous call to the police.'

'My God,' says Prasad, aghast. 'This is a new level of evil. How did they manage to avoid the watchmen?'

'I think the watchmen were paid off to be away from their posts for some time while the MLA's men came and went. They thought of everything. My concern is the girl, Mr Prasad. She is the only person who can tell us what may have happened. But also, if she saw something, her life could be in danger.'

'That's true. I'm going to focus on finding her. At least her I must protect and care for now,' says Prasad.

'Sir, my hands are tied, being within the force. I cannot go against my bosses. And DGP Bhaskar is not a man to cross. It would be dangerous. But you have connections. Surely you can make a few calls and see that something is done.'

'This is unbelievable, Varma. We came to the police for justice and here the police is coming to us for help. I cannot believe what I am hearing. This same DGP came to Raju's house and said, "I am here as a father" and God knows what else. And he himself is leading the coverup? Of course I won't let it be. Raju is beyond help now, but I'll fight for Archana and Shalini. Their names must be cleared.'

Varma can see that Prasad is tired and fired up at the same time. Just then, his phone rings and he excuses himself to take the call.

When he returns, he slumps back on his chair and says glumly, 'Well, they are moving fast. That was a contact of mine in the department. I am being transferred out of Karnataka. The papers are being drawn up and will be sent to me in the next couple of hours.

'See, Mr Prasad, this is what we face. How can anyone fight against this? I just went to the DGP to seek clarification. And already I have been marked out as a troublemaker and am being sent away.'

'Well, they can't shut me up,' Prasad says resolutely. 'I can fight, and I will.'

## 14

When Prasad calls Salve to tell him about the conversation with SI Varma, the lawyer informs him that they have two separate cases to deal with. The rape case, and now the murder case.

Although sympathetic, Salve is quite sure that in the first instance, without a victim, and the likelihood that evidence has been destroyed, there is pretty much no case. Unless one of the boys who did it comes forward.

The murder case is a different matter altogether. They have the body, the knife with Archana's fingerprints, and a suitcase full of cash. Means, motive, opportunity. A more open-and-shut case would be hard to find.

'I want to be heard, Salve. I want that bastard to be hurt. He cannot and should not get away with this,' Prasad says.

'Yes, we can hurt him, but you know what they say about a wounded tiger.'

Salve is of the opinion that with the cops and politicians joining forces to bury the original crime, it will be very hard to get the courts to view it differently. Besides, they have created a new crime to replace the original one.

'I've heard of people substituting witnesses, but here they've substituted a crime for a crime. Give me some time to draw up a draft of the petition. I'll send it to you tonight. And lie low, Prasad. These people are dangerous, so play it safe. We'll file the petition tomorrow and then take it one step at a time.'

Prasad is not entirely convinced about this approach but can't think of an alternative. As he drives home later in the evening, he becomes agitated again. How can he just sit around waiting for a petition to be filed? It could take days. In the meantime, Archana will have to remain in jail and Shalu is still to be found.

With his mind made up, Prasad turns towards the offices of *Bangalore Express*. The local newspaper is known for its daring investigations and hard-hitting headlines. The editor, Shashank

Ganguly, owes him a few favours and this is as good a time as any to call them in.

'Ganguly, I have a mega scoop for you,' Prasad says as he steps into the editor's office. He tells him the full story, from the events outside the Malibu club to his meeting with SI Varma.

Ganguly listens goggle-eyed. He can smell a huge opportunity, a front-page hit he hasn't had in a long while. Nanjundaswamy's name evokes fear in every heart, not only because of his ruthless tactics but also his violent temper and uncouth behaviour. It is public knowledge that he is plotting his path to chief ministership. Ganguly has been due a big juicy story on the man, and this is exactly it.

Meeting Ganguly makes Prasad feel a lot calmer. He is sure that in a few hours, when the story appears online, there will be chaos. The DGP will have some answering to do, as will the MLA.

It has been a long, hard day. He has earned himself a beer. Rather than going home, he drives to the Taj on MG Road to get a drink and enjoy his favourite club sandwich. He could use the time to consider how to go about locating Shalini. None of her friends has seen or heard from her. Her phone is at home, so there's no way of tracking her. If Varma has had any news, surely he would have called. But there has been nothing from him either.

Shalini's presence could help strengthen her mother's case and bring attention back to Nanjundaswamy. Where could she have gone, and how? He thinks of her pale, distraught face and bruised body, and feels something break inside him. Too much has happened, too quickly. Nothing makes sense anymore.

He looks up gratefully as a waiter places a tall, frothy glass of draft beer in front of him. That's when the phone rings. It's Ganguly.

'Yes, Ganguly? All done?'

'Sorry, Prasad. The story is not going to run.'

'Why? What happened? You owe me, Ganguly. And you know the story has substance, it could sell for you!'

'Don't you think I know that, Prasad? But management will not let it run. Nanjundaswamy is close to the ruling party leaders. Very close. And any story that shows him in a bad light doesn't have a chance of running. My bosses would hate to get on the wrong side of him. Sorry, Prasad. I wish I could help.'

'You are useless, Ganguly. Useless!'

Angrily, Prasad hangs up and starts making calls to some other journalists, who are all very excited till they find out who is involved.

After that, there is a distinct cooling off. They all promise to get back, but Prasad knows that nothing will happen.

He drains his glass of beer, pays and leaves the Taj. As he gets into the car and turns towards Ulsoor lake, he allows himself to hope that Janet will come up with some ideas. Personally, he is beat. All he wants to do is get home and collapse into bed, and just never wake up.

## 15

### Film Producer in Critical Condition, Suspects Escape Scene of Fatal Crash

A night out ended in tragedy for film producer Prasad Rao when an altercation erupted following a minor car accident. A two-wheeler reportedly scraped Rao's SUV at a traffic light, prompting a fiery exchange of words between the two parties. Those on the two-wheeler proceeded to beat Rao with bats before fleeing the scene. The critically injured victim was taken to St Martha's hospital, where he remains in a coma. CCTV footage from the area is being studied for further information as authorities work to apprehend those responsible for the crime.

# Part II

# 1

Bangalore Central Jail is going to be her home forever. That is the one thought that spins round and round in her head as Archana tries to get through another day without losing her sanity. The high walls topped with barbed wires keep her away from the world she knows. Inside these walls is her new universe. This is where she has to start again. But this time, all alone.

She knew she had stepped into a different world the moment they loaded her onto the prison bus. Handcuffed and under the watch of policemen with guns, unsmiling and unhelpful. When she struggled to climb the first step into the bus, no one bothered to help. Instead, someone tugged the chain tying her to the other prisoners and dragged her inside.

On reaching the prison, the first thing they did was to strip her naked so they could check if she had any prior injuries or was smuggling anything in. She cringed, standing unclothed in front of strangers who seemed completely indifferent to her state as they prodded her orifices. Then she was given a white salwar kameez and a set of underwear. Everything looked old and unwashed. But she pulled them on mechanically, struggling to suppress the rising nausea.

The jail was full of criminals who were here for many reasons, but there were very few who were in for murder. That gave her a special status, as one of the policemen took pains to tell her. The status of someone who needed to be watched over carefully, for she could be dangerous. After all, if you had killed once, you could easily kill again.

She was first taken to the superintendent's office. She stood before the middle-aged man with a huge potbelly and full head of hair, who looked up from behind his large wooden desk piled high with papers on seeing her.

'Mrs Gowda. Mrs Archana Gowda,' he said. The words came out in a rush. 'Murderer. Killed your own husband? What sort of woman are you? Hiding behind this innocent face. I want you to know that everything you want to do here is controlled by me. The rules are very simple. Do as you are told. No talking back. No questions. Jail is not the punishment for your crime. What happens in the jail will be your real punishment.'

'Take her away,' he said to the guards who had accompanied her.

As they walked down a dark, dimly lit corridor between high stone walls, they passed other doors, closed tight with small viewing slits that she assumed were for the guards to peer through. Somewhere in the distance were windows through which some daylight bounced in. The air was yellow with dust, making it hard to see. What light there was emanated from dim yellow bulbs hidden behind meshes. The stone floor felt cold and filthy to her bare feet.

At the end of the corridor, they came to a fork. The short path to the left led to a small single-storeyed building. She would find out later that the male prisoners were housed in the same compound, but in a bigger building on the other side. The two groups never met, for their own safety. The women's block looked even darker and sadder than the corridor, if that was possible. No windows, just a few grimy skylights high up in the ceiling. There was no way to tell if it was night or day.

'Because you are here for murder and you are new, you will be put in solitary for one month to help you get used to jail. After one month, you will be assigned a cell that you will share with others,' the taller of the two guards informed her.

'Breakfast, lunch and dinner will be brought to your cell. At 11 a.m. and at 4 p.m. you will be taken to the yard to walk around and get some sunshine. Otherwise, you will be in your cell. Here,' she said, pushing open a huge iron door with an echoing creak.

It was a small, dark room with a cot taking up much of the space. Archana could make out the outlines of a steel basin and a squat toilet that seemed to occupy the rest of the cell. About ten feet up was a small grilled window. Not wide enough for even a monkey to go through. The smell was overpowering, of faeces, urine and sweat. Like standing next to a sewer or septic tank. Perhaps there were rats here as well. Archana shuddered. Only a dim light from a yellow bulb ensured that it was not pitch dark.

'Ok. We're leaving now. You missed lunch, so the next meal will be dinner at 7 o'clock. At 4 p.m. one of the guards assigned to this floor will lead you to the open area for half an hour of exercise.'

With that the two guards banged the door shut behind them. Archana heard three big bolts being dragged into place and their footsteps faded away in the distance. Then there was silence. Nothing except the sound of her own breathing. She had never known silence like this.

Taking a tentative step forward in the impenetrable darkness, she reached the cot and collapsed on it, exhausted. As stiff and unforgiving as the prison bed was, it was still a refuge. And nothing seemed to matter really. She would be swallowed up by this gloomy place. Her life was over.

She lay back, and the dam burst. All the emotions that she had bottled up for the past eight months escaped in heaving sobs. Raju gone. Shalu gone. Why was God punishing her like this? She had done everything right, hadn't she? Every prayer. Every festival. Was this a test? But what was the point of passing this test? What was there to live for? Please God, she prayed, please let me die. Be kind to me.

## 2

'The bloody idiots have turned the jammers on again!' Fakii curses in Kannada. 'Some useless VIP must be visiting us today.'

Five-and-a-half-foot tall Fakii rules over all the other women in the jail. Her muscular body and shaved head make for an arresting sight. Angry-looking eyebrows arch across her forehead like thick black slashes on white paper. An incident involving several inmates with razor blades has left her with long scars across her cheeks. Even the male guards are afraid of this woman.

And this gives her many privileges, including access to a phone. With it, she conducts her extortion business from the jail. Though she can get away with almost anything, Fakii is disciplined about the use of her phone. An hour each morning, starting at 7 o'clock, and another hour at night, between eight and nine, are reserved for calls. That's when she raps out instructions for people to be kidnapped, shops to be held up, money to be collected and paid remotely.

Archana bumps into Fakii, literally, in her third month in the jail. She is distracted as she walks in the yard and does not see Fakii's outstretched leg. She takes a tumble and before she can recover from the shock and pain of the fall, Fakii is on her. She sits on her and leans into her face with a snarl. Her breath reeks of tobacco leaf and decay, of stale saliva and unbrushed teeth.

'Blind or what, you rande? What if you had hurt me?'

'I, I …' Archana mumbles, terrified.

'What I, I …' Fakii lifts Archana up and slaps her across the face. As she reels back in pain, Fakii pushes her so hard that she falls down again. A few others join in, raining kicks and blows on her shrinking body. Then Fakii stops them and bends down to examine her for a moment. 'This is not over, slave,' she says and walks away with her troops.

It seems to Archana that at every turn, there is some sort of punishment God has reserved specially for her. So far, she has been stripped and caned on at least four different occasions for no reason at all. She has been slapped, spat on, humiliated in every way possible, forced to go to bed without food, clean dirty toilets, swab the prison floors. Her body is marred by welts and bruises, her back crisscrossed with scars, her breasts carry welts from a ruler. The whites of her eyes have turned a pale pink, the lids red and swollen. She can still feel the hot lash of the cane on her bare shoulders and buttocks, the sting that would last an entire day, sometimes even longer.

At every turn, there is a beating or a punishment. And no one to call her own, not a single person. No place to call home either. She is alone, completely alone. She is dust, and she could perish any second.

Of them all, Fakii has taken a special liking for her. She slaps her for entertainment. Trips her as she walks by. Archana is Fakii's slave during the breaks and mealtimes. It is her duty to feed

Fakii. Sometimes, by the time Fakii has finished swapping stories with other prisoners and eating, there is no time for Archana to get any food.

If God created hell, surely this must be it, she thinks.

## 3

Then, one morning, something unexpected happens. Archana is standing, shoulders hunched in obeisance to Fakii, when she hears the other woman grumble about the jammers.

Without thinking, she blurts out, 'Hash Star Hash Seven.'

'What did you say?' Fakii snaps. 'Did I ask you to open your mouth?' She raises her hand as if to slap Archana.

'No, no, no,' Archana says hastily. 'That's how you can bypass the jammer.'

Fakii stops mid-motion. She frowns thoughtfully.

'Are you saying that if I press those things you say, I won't be bothered by the jammers?'

'Ye … ye … yes,' stammers Archana.

'And how the hell do you know this?' someone in Fakii's gang asks.

'I was doing some work with mobile phones before … before all this,' Archana says, tears springing to her eyes.

'Ok, stop all the crying and drama and tell me again what I need to do,' Fakii commands.

'Hash Star Hash Seven.'

'It's working,' Fakii exclaims excitedly. 'Hey, rande, you saved me today. Let me make these calls and then you and I are going to have a talk.'

And just like that, Archana's life changes.

The next day, Fakii clears out the yard space around her and spends an hour listening to Archana. Why she is here, who is responsible for what happened, the court case, Shalu's disappearance, all of it.

Fakii has been in jail for over eleven years, with no hope of getting out, for having gruesomely killed four people with a machete. She has seen and heard it all. She tells Archana that more than half the people in prison are like her, jailed for a crime they did not commit. Incompetent defence lawyers, corrupt policemen and an inefficient judiciary are responsible for people being locked away for years with no one to ask after them. However, Archana's case is unusual in that she is from the upper strata of society. Usually, that lot manages to stay out of prison. But if Nanjundaswamy is the opposition, then jail is a soft punishment, Fakii tells her. It's not often his enemies are left alive to tell their side of the story.

Fakii has no time for weaklings. Her whole life has been about fighting to get what she feels is owed to her. Her own parents have disowned her and now the prison gang is her family. She looks after them and they protect her.

To her, Archana is just another weakling. Cocooned in her little bubble of English education, a well-paying job and genteel aspirations. These may be strengths on the outside. But in jail they mark you out for bullying.

'So, what are you doing about it?' Fakii asks contemptuously.

'Doing about what?' asks Archana, puzzled.

'These people who did all this to you and your family. Are you going to let them get away with it? Are you just going to sit here and moan? The world is full of people who complain about things that have happened to them.'

'Those people have already won. I have no family left. No friends. I am sentenced to be here for twenty years. What do you want me to do? For what purpose? This is God's wish. I must have done something really bad in my previous life to deserve this.'

'Nonsense! Everyone makes their own future. You can't sit back and expect that things will happen on their own. I am tired of cowards who blame God for everything that goes wrong. They just don't want to take matters into their own hands. Taking control of your life is a choice. Why does God have to look after you? Can't you look after yourself? Don't you have two hands, two legs, and a brain between your ears? The Quran says one must believe and uphold justice even if it's against yourself, your parents, or your close relatives. And the Bhagavad Gita says it's one's dharma to fight against evil, doesn't it? Even if it's against your own family. In fact, sometimes, to fight evil, you have to become evil yourself. For the sake of your family, and especially for your daughter, you must fight. No one else is going to fight for you.'

'But what is the point of that? It won't bring my family back.'

'Lord Krishna says, don't be attached to the fruits of your actions. It's the intent that is important. Did he not say that?'

She looks at Archana's bewildered face and grimaces.

'Just because I'm here and I look like this, don't assume I'm not like you. I was not born with knives or these scars. Like you, I had a mother and father. And if you must know, the Quran is our holy book but my parents insisted that I was familiar with the Bible and the Gita too. When we were very young, dinner time in our home was full of arguments and debates about what the books said. We would disagree with something we read and my mother would patiently explain what the words actually meant. We did not have much, but we had a rich life.'

She is quiet for a while, then says, 'They had plans for me, but then other things happened, and here I am. I still remember some of those learnings, though. Importantly, I know that unless you fight for your rights and for whatever is yours, someone will push you out of the way. It's the way of the world. Of course, you can spend your time in jail crying and being upset and blaming God and fate. But no one cares.'

'I've lost everything I had. I have no idea what I can do,' Archana says.

Fakii sounds irritated now. 'For God's sake, stop feeling sorry for yourself. And start looking after your body. Eat properly. Stand in the sun when you can. Walk as much as you can. You need to be strong to stay alive in this jail. And you have a long life waiting for you outside as well. Self-help is the best help,' she says, her voice ringing loud and clear as she walks away to her cell for her afternoon nap.

## 4

Archana is suddenly transported to a different life. No more beatings or cussing. She sits at the table like a normal person and eats her food. Fakii finds herself someone else to slave drive.

It is amazing what a difference eating three times a day can make. Her bony body starts filling out. Her skin feels softer. The dark spots on it seem to be fading. Gradually, Archana begins to look more like the person she was when she entered the prison a year ago. Gone are the reddish-yellow eyes. Her bruises start healing, though yellow patches remain in multiple places. She loses the limp and walks straighter.

In a few months, a new Archana emerges. Thinner. Much thinner. Her cheeks are still sallow, but she looks and feels healthier. Each time she looks at herself in the mirror, she hopes that the protective shield Fakii has thrown over her stays intact. Getting out is a long way away and she will need all the protection she can get till then.

In a perverse sort of way, Archana misses the abuse and the beatings. They caused her so much pain that she had no time to miss her past life or even think about Raju and Shalu. Now the void threatens to take over. Tears well up each time she recalls their life together. Memories of a holiday or a meal or even an argument are enough to trigger a meltdown. The trivial things she once took for granted have become precious and she remembers and stores them away to savour in the lonely nights.

Her relationship with Fakii is dramatically different now. She has become Fakii's mobile help desk. Any issues with her phone, or the network, and Archana is immediately called for. They don't spend much time together, except as needed. But word quickly gets around that Archana is to be left alone. Even the guards who enjoy beating the women for no reason and grope them as they walk past get the message.

Her prison duties too change. From washing toilets, she is moved to the kitchen. A much coveted location. Occasionally, a jailor needs help with writing reports to be sent to the home ministry or organising expenses in a file on the computer. Once, she writes up a proposal requesting additional funds, which the warden sends upwards, and it actually meets with success, bringing a message of thanks from the big man himself, a very rare occurrence. It doesn't take her long to realise that there are many people in jail with physical skills but very few, if any, understand technology or know how to operate computers or create spreadsheets.

Sometimes, at night, before falling asleep, Archana thinks of that first conversation with Fakii, about revenge. She has been brought up to believe that people pay for their sins. That God operates in mysterious ways, but eventually good things happen to good people and bad people get punished. And it's impossible to go against His wishes, for isn't he the Annadata, the Karyakarta?

Anyway, she is to be in jail for another nineteen years. Even after she gets out, she is just one woman. The MLA has a whole army. No, revenge is a fantasy. Let God do his thing.

And so the days pass, and the years.

## 5

The day that makes her rethink all that she has been brought up to believe dawns like any other.

When someone tells her she has a visitor, Archana is sure it's a mistake. In the past five years no one has even called her, let alone visited. It occurs to her that even if someone tried, they may have been fobbed off.

As she walks towards the cubicle, Archana stares at the woman in a blue salwar-kameez who is already seated there, behind the glass partition. White shoulder-length hair. Spider lines emerging from the sides of her eyes and darting down her face. Thin lips. Archana frowns at the visitor, once again sure that this is a case of mistaken identity.

'Archu,' mouths the woman silently as she stands up slowly.

One word that brings the buried memories hurtling up.

'Janet?'

The woman nods and starts crying wordlessly.

Archana is shocked to see her old friend in this state. Janet looks twenty years older than when she last saw her. What has happened to her?

Archana reaches for the phone on her side of the cubicle.

'Janet, what happened? What's going on?' she asks, racked with emotion. There is tremendous joy at seeing her friend. And sadness at the state she is in.

Janet tries to get a grip on herself. 'I am sorry, Archu. I am so sorry. I don't have anything to say but sorry. For everything. For what happened to Raju, to Shalu, to you. So much happened, so soon. We are all still in shock.'

'It's been nearly five years, Janet. I'm slowly coming to terms with life here. I'm not going to lie. It's as hard as anything can be. And sometimes worse,' Archana says sadly. There is no need to hide anything from her best friend.

'I cannot believe our lives have changed so much and so suddenly. I still remember that evening at your house when Raju poured me a glass of wine. Who knew that would be our last time together?'

'How did you manage to get in here? Who did you have to call? What strings did you have to pull?'

'Pulled in some big favours, Archu. I just had to see you. Five years is the longest that I have not seen you since we first met. So here I am.'

'Do you have any news at all about Shalu? Has she been found? Did she contact you? I've been worried sick about her. You two were so close. You must know something.'

'No, Archu. It's like Shalu just vanished into thin air. No one knows where she is. She is not in touch with anyone. With Prasad being the way he is, and her grandparents long gone, no one is looking for her either.'

Archana's heart sinks at this news. She had hoped that somehow Shalu had been found and was well.

'We have to find her, Janet. We can't just give up on her like this. We have to do everything in our power to help her,' she says plaintively.

'But how, Archu? We don't even know where to start looking,' Janet says, wiping her tears.

'You'll have to start by going back to the beginning. To the night when Raju died. Maybe there's something we missed. You have to talk to everyone who was there that night and see if they remember anything that might help us.'

'I promise to keep looking, Archu. I will.'

'You must, and when you find her, keep her with you. Prasad and you are family. Bring her up like she is yours.' She paused. 'How is Prasad? How are you doing? Tell me everything.'

'You know that Prasad had an accident a few days after Raju …'

'Yes, I heard about it. Near Ulsoor lake. He got into a fight with some bikers, no?' Archana responds, thinking back to the day Fakii had found out about the accident through her vast network of operatives.

'It turns out that Prasad's accident was not an accident. It was a message from Nanjundaswamy. Prasad was beaten so badly that he was in a coma for two weeks. He broke his spine and will be bedridden forever. He has only ten per cent vision in one eye and his hearing is considerably diminished. Obviously, we are not working anymore. We sold our house and moved to JP Nagar, where we live in a two-bedroom apartment with a full-time nurse. He asks about you all the time. But there's nothing he is able to do. I can't even leave him alone as he is too much for one nurse to handle. His brother has come to spend a few days with us, so I could get away to see you, Archu.'

Archana leans forward slowly and presses her hands flat against the glass partition. Janet mirrors the gesture on the other side of the glass. A 3.5 mm pane cannot keep their emotions from connecting in this moment of naked vulnerability.

'Both our lives destroyed by that man, just to save his son. There is a hell waiting for him. I hope he gets there sooner than later.'

'Not just that, Archu. Tabassum's father, Anthony's father and many others have been threatened or beaten into silence. It's been horrible. Everyone has gone into their shells. And what is worse, Nanjundaswamy has become a minister.'

The man is capable of boundless evil, Archana thinks, as she looks at her grieving friend.

Janet's visit throws Archana into a melancholic mood. She lies in her bed staring at the cobwebbed ceiling. No one she knows seems to be around anymore. The threats have done their job. Has Shalu been silenced too? With the DGP on Nanjundaswamy's side, how long will she be able to hide? And when they find her, what will they do to her? Archana cannot bring herself to think of it.

# 6

A few days after Janet has come and gone, Archana is surprised by another visitor.

This time, there is a man waiting for her. A man she has met only a couple of times, but whose face is imprinted in her memory.

'How do you have the courage to come and see me, SI Varma? Have you come to check if I am still alive?'

Varma rises from his chair awkwardly and looks away to hide his discomfort. The guard looks like she is ready to intervene if necessary.

Not for the first time, Varma wonders if he has done the wrong thing in coming to meet Archana. His former boss, DGP Bhaskar, is now the IG, and if he gets to hear of this visit, there will be consequences. But he has a message to convey and his conscience will not allow him to leave the task undone.

He takes a deep breath. 'Please hear me out, Mrs Gowda.'

Archana is undecided, but she sits down facing him.

Varma takes the chair opposite her and begins, 'Mrs Gowda, you are right to feel the way you do. The police have let you down. The system has let you down. Yes, I've let you down too. But it's not what you think. Maybe I should have fought harder instead of trying to keep my job, but beyond that, I am not guilty of anything. I spoke to Mr Prasad before ... before his accident.'

'Not accident, Varma. It was intentional.'

'I suspected as much, but there's no proof. When I met Mr Prasad, I told him everything I knew, but I had no evidence for it.'

Systematically, he lays out everything he knows about that night. Shalu leaving the house. The men coming in. The chloroform, the murder, Archana's arrest.

'Without any evidence, this is just a theory. Then I myself got threatened by the DGP. So I kept quiet. Anyway, what good would my poking around have done, I thought. If there's no proof, it didn't matter. Then I got transferred to the Railways, where I still am. As long as IG Bhaskar is posted here, I won't be allowed to come back to Crime.'

Archana struggles to revise her opinion of her visitor. She was never one for cynicism, but her time in jail has wrung out all traces of optimism. She assumes the worst. She expects the worst. And in her first few years in jail, she was not disappointed. These last few months, however, have been a different experience altogether.

'Mrs Gowda, Mrs Gowda …' Varma's voice interrupts her thoughts.

'Sorry, I got lost there for a moment. Do you want to ask me something? I'm still not sure why you are here.'

'I don't want to prolong this, Mrs Gowda, but I wanted you to know that your daughter, Shalini, has been located.'

Nothing could have prepared Archana for this. While she hoped that Shalu had somehow survived, she had half suspected that Nanjundaswamy had already found her. She had never dared to think beyond that.

She half rises from her seat in excitement. 'Where? How is she? How did you find her?'

'From the time I left Bangalore, I've been trying to track her down. I thought this was the very least I could do, and if needed, I could protect her from Nanjundaswamy's goons. But I worried needlessly. You have a very smart daughter, Mrs Gowda. The night she ran away from home, she went to the church that Mrs Janet Rao goes to. She met one of the nuns there and after hearing her story, they quietly absorbed her into the convent adjacent to the church. As there is no case against her, the nuns have committed no crime. They sent her to a convent in Coonoor, and from there she went to a local college. She has completed her Masters and is planning to teach in a local school. She stays in the convent itself. And I am told that she is fine, at least physically.'

Archana is beside herself with joy. Shalu has been found. She is safe. She is in college and will soon start a job. She feels like laughing and crying at the same time. It is an emotion she never thought to experience again.

'Do you have a number for the convent? I want to speak to her. She needs to understand what happened. There's so much to explain to her. She must be worried about me.' The words rush out in a torrent of relief and anxiety.

'Yes, Mrs Gowda. I do,' he replies.

'Please say the number slowly so that I can memorise it.'

Varma repeats the number three times until Archana has committed it to her memory.

Someone knocks on the door to let Varma know that the time for this unofficial visit is up. He nods and stands up to leave.

'Thank you so much, Varma. You've brought the only spark of happiness into my life in the last five years. I pray that God gives you whatever you want. May your troubles get washed away. God bless you.'

'I am sorry, Mrs Gowda, about everything that's happened to you. But now you have something to look forward to. Someone will be waiting for you when you get out. I don't think she is in any danger from Nanjundaswamy or his goons because she poses no danger to anyone. Anyway, for them, it's old news. But please don't tell anyone about my coming to see you here. I don't want IG Bhaskar to get inquisitive.'

He pushes back his chair and gets up.

'I'll take your leave now. If I can help in any way, please let me know. The superintendent here was my teacher at the police academy in Mysore, which is how I was able to meet you. If you need to contact me, please just leave a message with him, he'll pass it on to me.'

Varma walks out of the room, leaving Archana to soak in the news. Shalu has been found. How is she doing, though? What does she look like as an adult? Does she miss her at all?

There is only one way to find out.

## 7

'Who was it that came to meet you?' Fakii asks, watching Archana return to the cells with a bounce in her step.

'You won't believe it, but Shalu has been found. She's alive and in Coonoor. Give me your phone. I need to call her.'

'Arre, don't get too excited. Stop and think for a minute. Remember, as far as your daughter is concerned, you are a murderer. That's what the newspapers said, right? You don't know how she reacted to that. Also, it's been five years since you got here. A lot may have happened in her life since then. You don't know how she feels about you today.'

'She's my daughter. She knows me. She knows what I can and cannot do. She must be missing me. Five years is a long time for a child. Imagine living in a convent with strangers,' Archana responds as she punches in the number she has learnt by heart.

'Hello, this is Mother Mary Convent,' comes a woman's voice.

'Can I speak to Shalu, please? Shalini. Shalini Gowda,' Archana says, the words leaping out of her.

'Madam, there is no Shalini here.'

'What? Are you sure? I was told that she stays here. Can you please check?'

'Madam, I am sure. But call around 7 p.m. and speak to Sister Philomena. She may be able to help.'

'I don't understand. I'm sure Shalini stays here. Why are you saying she does not? Who is Sister Philomena?'

'Madam, I don't have the answers to your questions. Please call in the evening and ask for Sister Philomena. Thank you.'

With that, the line is disconnected.

Could Varma have got it wrong? Is Shalu no longer at the convent? But he was so sure about it. Archana consoles herself with the thought that at least she has the name of someone there who might help. She checks the time. It's only 3 p.m. Seven feels like a lifetime away.

Fakii has to remind Archana to keep calm and not call earlier than she has been told to. 'If they said seven, wait till seven. Don't call earlier and create more tension. And are you prepared for Shalu not being there at all?'

'No, don't say that, Fakii. Not even as a joke. She has to be there. Varma cannot be wrong.'

At the stroke of seven, Archana takes the phone from Fakii and goes to a quiet corner in the yard. She redials the number she had called a few hours earlier.

The same voice says, 'Mother Mary Convent.'

'Hello. Yes, I had called earlier for Shalini. This is her mother, Archana. Can I talk to Sister Philomena?' Archana's heart is in her mouth as she speaks into the phone.

'Yes, madam. Just a minute.'

Archana's heart starts beating faster. Who is Sister Philomena? Does she know where Shalu is? Why this runaround in the first place?

A few seconds and a click later, 'Hello' comes a woman's voice down the line.

'Hello,' says Archana again. 'I had called for Shalini, Shalini Gowda, in the afternoon and I was told that I should call and talk to Sister Philomena. Is that you, Sister?'

'Yes, I was informed. May I know who is speaking?'

'This is Archana. Her mother.'

'I see. And where are you calling from?'

'How does it matter to you? Just let me speak to my daughter.' Archana is beginning to lose patience.

'I am sorry, Mrs Gowda. I don't think that's a good idea.'

'Who are you to decide if it's a good idea for me to talk to my daughter or not?'

'Mrs Gowda, I am Sister Philomena. I run the convent here. Sister Beatrice and I are the ones who brought Shalu to Coonoor,' the voice says gently. 'It has been over five years now, and while she seems to have settled down, she's still very fragile and anxious about her surroundings and about talking to people. We don't want to take the chance that hearing from you will cause her further distress.'

'But I am her mother!'

'I completely understand, Mrs Gowda. But it has taken a lot of effort and attention on our part to get Shalu to a stable condition. When she came to us, she was broken. She cried and sat in her room without speaking to anyone for days. Not eating or drinking. The sisters in the convent slowly coaxed her to come out of her shell and start engaging with the world. We are very protective of her.'

'But …'

'Mrs Gowda, we both want what is best for her. You are her mother and we are her local guardians. We believe that, in time, we will get the old Shalu back. Just, not yet. I am sure you don't want to take a risk with her health now. And for no good reason, because anyway, she still can't come to see you, right? We don't know who is watching.'

'But I want her to know that I am innocent,' Archana insists.

'The good Lord knows you are. I know you are.'

'How do you know?'

'That inspector was here, Mrs Gowda. He told me everything.'

So, SI Varma did go well beyond his duty in checking on Shalu. Maybe he is a good man after all. With all that has happened in the past few years, it has become hard for her to tell the good from the bad.

'Mrs Gowda, I have devoted my life to serving the Lord and I have realised He operates in mysterious ways. Many times, we just don't understand His plans. But there is always a reason for everything. I pray that the truth comes out someday soon.'

Archana feels the tears start again.

'Sorry, I am sorry,' she says, her voice trembling.

'Don't worry about Shalu, Mrs Gowda. She is one of us now. We love her almost as much as you do. Allow us to look after her until you come to take her back. This must be what the good Lord intended for us. To restore a child to her mother.'

Archana sobs into the phone. 'Thank you, Sister. I miss her terribly, I just want to hear her voice once. But I don't want to cause her any more suffering. Will you please continue to look after her for me? And if you don't mind, can I call you once in a while? Not often. Maybe once in a few months, to hear about her?'

'Yes, of course, Mrs Gowda.' Sister Philomena proceeds to tell Archana about Shalu's college, the subjects she studied, the school she is going to start teaching at, and how she spends her time in the convent.

Twenty minutes later, a very weepy Archana returns to Fakii and hands the phone back.

'Spoke to her?' asks Fakii, looking into Archana's eyes.

Archana shakes her head tearfully.

'Oh, for heaven's sake, don't start again. It's not going to change anything, is it? Stop crying and think of something productive to do. I've told you enough times, you need to think about getting out and finding those guys. Make them pay for what they did. Tears are just a waste of time.'

## 8

Archana is filled with a new energy after talking to Sister Philomena. Hope is on the horizon again.

Two days later, Fakii wordlessly hands her phone to Archana. The image on the screen is of a beautiful, cheerful face, bathed in the warm rays of the sun. Her eyes twinkle with joy as the sun's light streams across her skin. She is looking up towards the sky and pointing at something. Her curly hair is bunched up at the back of her head.

Shalini.

She has changed so much in these years. She has become even more beautiful. Radiant.

The clouds of despondency clear. She has lost Raju, but she still has Shalu. And she seems to be well looked after.

That's when Archana takes the silent vow that will see her through the rest of her time in jail. She will live for Shalini. And she will begin to think about what Fakii has been saying.

After that, every chat with Fakii ends up stoking the fire of revenge. They have been speaking about it for years, but now, even a stray comment or observation fuels Archana's anger. Why should anyone get away with committing such a heinous crime? If someone has done something wrong on earth, the punishment has to be delivered on earth. In this lifetime. That is real justice. Words to this effect are continuously drummed into Archana's head.

Of course, it's easy for Fakii to say these things. She grew up with violence around her. She has been part of a gang from her teens. She knows how this world operates. She knows how to win. And how to make people pay.

Archana, on the other hand, has never even got into a physical fight with anyone. No one she knows has been arrested by the police, not even for a white-collar crime. The only policemen she knows are the ones who arrested her, beat her, abused her. Apart from Varma, of course.

Before all this happened, she was just content to be wife and mother. Even when Shalu, Raju and she went on a drive, she would sit in the backseat and enjoy listening to father and daughter chatting away about inconsequential things. Once, when Raju took the wrong turn and got stuck, it was Shalu, all of eight years, who got out of the car and directed the traffic to get them back on the right road. Yes, Archana was never the fighting sort.

Time passes slowly. The numbing routine of jail—wake up, roll call, clean the cell, have tea at 6 a.m., bathe, breakfast at 7.30 a.m., work all morning in the kitchen, have lunch at 11.30, walk in the yard at 4, eat dinner at 6.30, then roll call and back to the cell—keeps her focused with no time to think of anything else. Occasionally, she gets a photograph from Sister Philomena. That gives her added energy for a few more days. Weeks even.

Then, one day, she gets a message that the jail superintendent wants to meet her. In the ten years she has been here, this is the first time he has summoned her. She still recalls with a shudder her first encounter with the previous superintendent when he warned her about her fate in the jail and how he would treat her should she break any of the rules. Since then, she has ensured that she does not step out of line, no matter what.

Everyone knows the superintendent never calls anyone unless there is good news or, more likely, bad news. Most people complete their prison sentence without meeting him even once.

Unsure of what to expect, Archana walks up to his office, accompanied by a guard.

'Mrs Gowda,' the superintendent greets her gently, his voice belying his size and large moustache, as Archana stands deferentially in front of him. 'I have a job for you.'

He pushes his mobile phone towards her.

'I hear you are a genius with phones. Can you set mine up so that I can read my daughter's messages from her phone?'

'Wh … what, sir?' Archana stutters in surprise. This is the last thing she expected, that the superintendent would summon her to ask for a favour.

'Why do you look surprised, Mrs Gowda? Superintendents have children too.'

'Yes, yes, sir. Sorry, sir.'

'Can this be done, Mrs Gowda?' he asks again.

'It can be done, sir. But you know it's illegal.'

'Mrs Gowda, circumventing our jammers is illegal too,' smiles the superintendent. 'We know everything that happens,' he says, noticing Archana's discomfited expression. 'We decide when to act, that's all.

'As for my daughter, yes, it's illegal, I know, but I think her husband is beating her and she is not telling us or doing anything about it either. If I could get into her phone, I could find out from her texts if something is wrong. Maybe she's talking to her friends. I really need to know. No matter how old she is, she's still my baby.' He does little to conceal the sadness in his eyes.

Archana is reminded of Raju and Shalu. He always said she would be her baby forever.

'I agree, sir. We should look after our babies. I can do better than what you are asking for, sir. I can activate her camera from your phone.'

'You can do what?' he asks, startled.

'I can set it up so that you can turn on her camera from here, then you can see whatever her phone sees. But be careful how you use it, sir, because you don't know what you will see and if you will be able to bear it,' she replies, parent-to-parent.

The superintendent stops to think, absentmindedly scratching his chin. After a few moments, he says, 'You are right, Mrs Gowda. I don't know if I can handle seeing everything. Let's just do the texts. If I find anything there, that is enough for me to act. I don't need to see it.'

Archana picks up the phone and concentrates on keying in instructions. She asks the superintendent for his daughter's number, which she keys in as well. A few minutes later, she hands the phone back to him.

'It's done, sir. For this to work, though, there needs to be a direct connection with her phone. The pairing has to happen, like with Bluetooth. But in this case, no authentication is needed. You just need to call her once, and when she answers, the connection will be made. After that, her messages will continually replicate on your phone. When you go to your messages, you will see hers appear in a different colour from yours. It will all be in one message folder. Makes it easier for you.'

'I'll call her as usual this evening and check. I'll send for you if there's a problem.'

He puts his phone away, gets up and walks around the table.

'Come, walk with me, Mrs Gowda.' He steps out of his office and she follows as he climbs up a flight of stairs to the roof of the prison. From there, they walk down a short corridor and on to an open-air terrace. The setting sun on the horizon bathes the earth as far as the eye can see in an eye-pleasing orange. There is some sort of habitation in the distance. Just outside the prison, life seems to go on as it once had for her. It takes her a moment to realise that this is her first exposure to the outside world since she was locked in ten years ago. It feels like she has walked into another world, one she didn't know existed until now, right outside the prison gate.

The terraces on both sides are enclosed by chain-link fencing, but there are gaps near the edges where she can see similar tracts of land running at right angles along all the four walls, and a few guards patrolling the perimeter. Below, on either side of her, is an exercise yard behind barbed wire fences. At the end of each yard runs a concrete wall, painted white, for protection against the normalcy of the outside world.

'This is the best view of the sunset anyone can have for miles. I come here sometimes to think, or just to clear the cobwebs in my mind. Mrs Gowda, I'll leave you here for fifteen minutes precisely. There's a flask with tea on that table there. Feel free to have a cup if you like. After fifteen minutes, a guard will come to take you back to your cell.'

As he turns to go, Archana asks, 'Why, sir? Why this treatment?'

'Inder spoke to me. Varma,' he clarifies, seeing the question on Archana's face. 'He gave me some details. He is convinced that you should not be here. He's junior to me, but I trust his judgement. Unfortunately, I don't make the rules. I only implement them.'

He walks away, leaving her alone on the terrace.

Archana pours herself a cup of tea. This is proper tea, not the hot liquid they get downstairs. Ten years since she has had a decent cup of tea.

She sips the tea and looks at the horizon.

There are two worlds, she thinks. A world where people like Fakii treat you like garbage and a world where you break bread together. A world where the superintendent gets his people to beat you up mercilessly and a world where he offers you tea and you sip it as you watch the sun go down. A world where innocent people get caught up in other people's crimes and a world where criminals suck innocent people into their criminal networks. A world where the police protect you from criminals and a world where the police are the criminals.

It's all a matter of luck, which world you inhabit. Most people live innocently in their own world, not knowing the other world could be waiting for them just round the corner. A little thing can tip you over into the other world. And that little thing is not in your control.

'Amma, Amma.'

Archana is brought back to reality with a thud.

'Amma, it's time,' the guard says politely.

'Oh, yes. Sorry.' Archana places the cup on the table and slowly walks back down the corridor and the steep flight of stairs to her real world.

## 9

'What did that dabba fellow want?' asks Fakii as Archana walks back into her cell block.

Very briefly, Archana tells Fakii about the mobile phone assistance required by the superintendent and the tea on the terrace.

'Waah, Archana. He must really like you,' Fakii says in a mocking sing-song voice, poking her in the ribs conspiratorially.

'Oh, come on now, Fakii. I am over fifty years old. An old hag. Waiting to die or get out in another ten years. That's my only goal. That, and to see Shalu.'

'I've heard that this superintendent is not as bad as the previous fellow. That kedi was corrupt and violent. And no one could say anything. You may have met him on your first day. This chap is much better. Very strict and wants everything to happen by the rules. He is not very popular with his bosses, but I think he has some protectors,' says Fakii. 'I am told he's due to retire in two or three years.'

While the beatings are in the past and the two are as friendly as could be, Archana is still a little afraid of Fakii. She has seen her temper and the violence she is capable of. So she takes nothing for granted.

On most days, the two women manage to grab five minutes together. And every few days Fakii has a new story about Nanjundaswamy, about something horrible he has done and got away with. Each time, Archana feels a bit of her heart hardening. There is so much injustice in the world and so few people fighting the evil in the system. But if this is what God wants his world to be, then it's up to Him to fix it as well. Anyway, what can she do on her own?

'You heard? Nanjundaswamy is going to become the next chief minister,' Fakii says, interrupting Archana's thoughts.

'What? Chief minister? How?' says Archana, surprised.

'What did you expect?' He has killed or destroyed all his opponents and made so much money for the party. This time next month, he will have been elected chief minister.'

'How does he get so much money? Do you know?' Archana has spent ten years in prison with convicted criminals. But she still knows nothing of their ways.

'How do you think? Nothing moves in the government without a bribe. Nothing. Roads, buildings, contracts, everything happens only if money is paid. To get a good job in any government department, you have to pay money. They also get money from every restaurant, bar and shop that is allowed to remain open, otherwise there are mysterious fires or other kinds of damage. Real-estate deals are big too. Of course, the biggest source of money is criminals. We all have to pay to be allowed to break the law and not get into trouble with the police. From top to bottom, everyone gets a share. Nanjundaswamy is expert at this.'

'Do you have to pay him too?' asks Archana.

'What kind of idiotic question is that? I pay him several lakhs every year. Not directly, but through his network. Finally, everything is managed by his right-hand man, that bewarsi Ajay.'

'Ajay,' repeats Archana softly.

'Do you know that bastard?' Fakii looks searchingly at Archana.

'Yes. He was the one who came home that last night, offering us cash to withdraw the case.'

'He's very smooth, but the most dangerous of them all, and he has Nanjundaswamy's full trust.' Fakii shakes her head in disgust. 'I think people are more afraid of him than of Nanjundaswamy. Cannot trust anything coming out of his mouth.'

'Oh, also, your friend,' Fakii says, 'IG Bhaskar, he is retiring this month.'

'That is some good news, I guess,' mutters Archana.

'It's good news only if you plan to do something with it. Otherwise, it's just something that happened in the world, with no connection to you.' Fakii is at it again, urging her to react.

With her mind in turmoil, Archana turns to physical activity to tire herself out and get some sleep at night. The regular yoga sessions that the jail organises have helped her maintain a sense of balance and ensured that she is not a wreck despite all this time in jail. But of late, even that isn't sufficient to bring her peace of mind. Some days, she doesn't want to see anyone or eat anything. Just lie in bed and cry.

But she keeps at it, walking as much as she can every day. She has even started doing push-ups at the end of the walk. She can do as many as three at a stretch, to the amusement of her cell mates. But a lifetime of no exercise cannot be changed in days. She isn't trying to be a muscle-bound woman, which would be quite impossible for a fifty-year-old woman in her state. She just wants to be fit enough for whatever awaits her in the world outside, whenever that time comes.

The infrequently sent photographs of Shalu continue to give her pleasure, but not like before. They make her miss her daughter even more. And Raju. Sometimes, without warning, a memory from the past makes her catch her breath, but she keeps her feelings firmly locked away. Prison is too dirty for those precious memories to be aired.

She is now nearly fifty-three, and has been inside for far too many years.

Through it all, the one thing that has kept her sane is her growing reputation as a tech expert. Her knowledge of mobile phones, although she hasn't even owned one for years, gives her an unspoken immunity in prison: everyone knows not to cross her. She often has to repair old, clunky handsets that are smuggled in and passed around; sometimes she even ends up helping someone in the men's side of the prison via the guards' network. Yet, there is only one person she can call a friend, and that's Fakii. The very person who caused her the most grief in the beginning has become her most trusted ally; one whose fear-inducing presence keeps everyone else from troubling her. And she cannot help but thank God for this.

## 10

The news about Prasad's death also filters in via Fakii. Apparently, he never recovered from the beating many years ago. Towards the end, he was completely bedridden, with his organs shutting down one by one. Finally, he had given up the fight and passed on.

Janet is now completely alone. Her family had abandoned her when she married out of the community all those years ago. And Prasad's family was never comfortable with a T-shirt-and-pants-wearing, churchgoing daughter-in-law. Not having children meant that the barrier had become a chasm over the years. Gradually, Raju and Archana had become the family they lost. Shalini, of course, was the icing on the cake.

Archana can't stop thinking about what Janet is going through. When she tells Fakii this, her resourceful friend comes up with a plan: she could apply for a furlough that will allow her to visit Janet.

Thus it is that, on a Thursday afternoon, nearly thirteen years after stepping into Bangalore Central Jail, Archana finds herself in a police jeep driving towards JP Nagar. For the occasion, she requests a sari that is given to convicts in special circumstances. A plain cotton sari in green. Not her favourite colour, but better than the usual jail wear. She has a good, long bath, ties her hair in a bun and sticks a bindi on her forehead. She doesn't want to embarrass Janet in front of whoever else may be at her place.

As the jeep turns into the road leading to Janet's new apartment, Archana asks the driver to stop a short distance away. She can only imagine the response from the residents of the society when they see her getting out of a police jeep. She would rather her visit is as discreet as possible and not draw attention to herself.

Since the furlough has been made possible due to the superintendent's intervention, the driver and the female guard are amenable to her request. Archana walks the few hundred metres to the entrance of the society, where she has to fill a register and have herself announced. Then she takes the lift up three floors and approaches Janet's apartment. The door stands slightly ajar, and a few shoes lie scattered on either side of the door. She can hear the murmur of hushed voices within. Visitors, no doubt. On seeing Archana, Janet jumps up from her chair and runs across the room. She pulls her into a fierce hug, her chest heaving with sobs.

The two friends stand in the doorway, crying. Archana holds Janet close. 'I am so sorry, Janet. So sorry.'

Finally, when Janet is able to compose herself, she leads Archana inside. A couple of neighbours who were keeping her company get up and mumble goodbye before leaving them alone.

'I should not say this, but I am glad he has gone, Archu. He suffered so much for so long. I want to always remember him as the energetic, fun-loving Prasad I knew and loved.'

Archana can understand that. Prasad always had enough energy for the five of them. To watch him as he lay in bed, unable to move or see or hear—it's the worst possible punishment anyone could have thought of for Janet.

'Nanjundaswamy has a lot to answer for,' she says quietly, sitting down beside Janet.

'Yes, he destroyed two families, didn't he? I hope he rots in hell. And here, on earth too. He left us with nothing.'

'Not nothing, Janet. We still have Shalu.'

'Shalu. We did try to find her, Archu, but had no luck. Now I'll have much more time to look for her. I promise that's what I'll dedicate my time to. To find Shalu.'

'Oh no, Janet. I know where she is.'

'You do?' Janet is taken aback. 'Then why are you keeping it to yourself? Tell me where she is. Let me go bring her here.'

'I don't know, Janet. I don't know if the time is right.' Archana fills her in on the conversation she had with Sister Philomena some years ago.

'How can Shalu be angry with you? Even if she is, once she hears the full story, she will want to be with you. And till you come home, she can stay with me. Let's try to put our family back together, Archu. What little we have left.'

'Janet, you think I don't want that too? But what if she doesn't believe me? It will be even worse than it is now. Not only did I kill her father, she will think I am lying about it. Also, I worry that her life will be in danger again, once Nanjundaswamy and his lot get to know that she is alive.'

'So what do we do, Archu? Just sit tight?'

Janet is asking the same question that Fakii has, so often. *What are you going to do?*

On the drive back, Archana sits quietly, deep in thought. If she does nothing, she'll probably lose Shalu forever. If she does something, she could lose her own life. Nanjundaswamy is not to be messed with, unless he can be pushed into a position from which he cannot retaliate. But how is a lone woman in jail supposed to make that happen? Yet, ironically, it is in jail that she has access to the most devious criminal minds. She asks herself wryly, do prisons rehabilitate people or educate them about the ways of the world? She herself was once a God-fearing, family-loving, mild-mannered woman. Not anymore. She came in innocent but will leave wise. And her trump card is Fakii.

# 11

'The superintendent wants to see you. Come with me.'

In all these years, this is only the second time she has been summoned. The previous time, it was to manipulate a mobile phone connection.

Archana follows the guard down the corridor to the superintendent's office. She enters and stands facing the superintendent, who is busy reading a document. He gestures towards a chair, indicating that she is to sit. But she remains standing awkwardly in the middle of the room.

He finishes doing whatever he needs to do with the document and looks up to see Archana still standing in front of his desk. He takes off his spectacles and cleans them with a light blue handkerchief, then puts them back on his nose.

'Please sit, Mrs Gowda. It's a request. If you prefer orders, then it's an order as well.'

Archana sits at the edge of the visitor's chair, wondering what plans the superintendent has for her. Astonishingly, a staff member walks in with a flask and two empty cups.

The superintendent reaches across and fills both the cups. He pushes one towards Archana and picks up the other. 'Please join me for tea,

Mrs Gowda,' he says. Then he looks at her and says, 'Mrs Gowda, firstly I want to say sorry.'

Archana nearly drops her cup in shock. Did he just say sorry? For what? Their paths have barely crossed and she cannot think of anything he may have done to her, or against her.

He puts his cup down and leans forward. 'I am sorry that you were sent here in the first place. And sorry that you are still here, paying for a crime you did not commit. Since the day you arrived, your behaviour has been exemplary. Never a complaint, even when you were being given the Fakii treatment. In fact, I continually hear stories of your kindness and willingness to help other prisoners. You are a good person, Mrs Gowda. A very good person. This is what I have seen with my own eyes.'

He pauses to take a sip of tea. 'Then there's what Inder said to me all those years ago. I have no doubt he was right. You're not a common criminal, Mrs Gowda. Not common. Not a criminal. And I am sorry that I ever thought you were.'

'Some more tea?' he asks as he refills his own cup.

Archana declines. Her mind is in a whirl, emotions tripping over each other as she listens to him.

'If you had been in the police or in a similar job for as long as I have been, you would know that one gets hardened over time. And in a jail you only get criminals sentenced by the court. Many of them are cruel and carry no guilt. Your friend Fakii is a case in point. She killed four people in cold blood and doesn't show a shade of remorse. So, it becomes the norm for us to see a criminal in everyone. It needs an Archana Gowda to show us what's wrong with the system. And to acknowledge that humanity exists, and that we should recognise it in everyone. No matter how hard it is.'

He stands up and paces the room as he continues, 'Mrs Gowda, I am retiring at the end of this month. It's time for me to go. I'll spend time with my grandchild—yes, my daughter's problems are in the past now—and learn to be a human being again. Before I go, I want you to know that I have made a strong recommendation for an early release for you. It will take a year or so, and is finally up to the prison board and the home ministry. But I am hopeful. And so should you be. Of course, there are no guarantees, but with your track record here, you should qualify.

'I have a parting gift for you. Our prison library has finally got some funds for an upgrade. We'll be installing two new computers and a high-speed internet connection in the women's wing. Everything will be monitored and tracked by the central server. But I have arranged for you to get an hour every day on the computer. I think your mobile phone skills will be much in demand in the future. But technology changes very fast. I hope you can use this time to upskill, so that when you get out, you can find something useful to do. I've signed the requisite forms.'

He stands up and folds his hands in a namaste. 'We may not meet again or even see each other again. I wish you well and hope that the future works out the way you want it to. You should start thinking about what you can do when you get out of here.'

He rings a bell to summon the guard.

Archana walks back to her cell in a daze. She hasn't said a word to the superintendent. Not even a thank you for the tea or the apology, or for recommending an early release.

## 12

An early release. Archana has not thought about what freedom might mean. Twenty years had seemed too long and the end too distant to make plans. And jails have strict routines which, while restrictive, give you something to do, to a set schedule. But several years of the same routine would now be blown away and she would have to start again in the outside world. She is not sure which is more dangerous. Outside or inside. There is no Fakii outside to protect her. Where will she go? What will she do? Where will she live? Should she ask the superintendent to take back his recommendation? It's one thing to visit Janet on furlough. To have a criminal living with her could have negative repercussions for Janet. But she knows no one anymore, besides Janet.

'Now what world are you lost in, you lazy cow?' Fakii interrupts her rumination.

Archana sits up on her mattress and tells Fakii about the meeting with the superintendent and the possibility of an early release. She is unsure how Fakii will react. Most people don't like good things to happen to other people. This is especially so in prison. Everyone wants everyone else to be equally miserable. You can see it clearly when a prisoner receives goodies from a visiting family member. Not only does the stuff vanish into the hands of the other prisoners, but the person who received it in the first place gets beaten up. 'You think you are better than us or what?'

Not surprisingly, most prisoners are afraid of getting anything worthwhile from their visitors and keep trying to return gifts. If that's impossible, they hand them to a guard, so that they themselves can return to their cells empty-handed.

But Fakii is different.

'That is the best news I've heard in a long time,' she exclaims gleefully. 'Sometimes, Allah ensures good things do happen to good people.'

'Fifteen years, Fakii. Don't forget that's what it will be by the time the approvals come through.'

'But it could have been twenty,' retorts Fakii. 'Twenty awful years. Which you have not had, thanks to me. Just imagine! In a couple of years, you could be out of this place.'

'Let's not get too excited. The superintendent only said he has made the recommendation. It still has to be accepted, and then the home ministry has to clear it.'

'If the superintendent told you this, he must expect that it will go through. Otherwise, he would never have said it. I am sure of it. You should assume that you will be out in two years,' Fakii says firmly. 'Stop being so negative.'

'Thirteen years is such a long time. I am so used to not having to think for myself, and just doing what someone tells me to do, to their timetable.

I don't know how I'll survive outside. How long will it take for me to adjust to this freedom? And all alone. When I came here, I didn't have any time to prepare. One day I was free, the next day I was not. Everything just happened. I had to adjust to a place I knew nothing about, overnight. Now I have time to get ready for a world I once knew.'

'So, what do you plan to do when you are out? How do you want to get ready for it?' asks Fakii.

'There are only two people I know outside, Fakii. Janet, my oldest friend. And Shalu. I'll rebuild my world around them.'

Shalu is still at the convent in Coonoor. The photographs sent to her trace the story of a girl who has graduated from college and become a teacher. A confident, happy young woman. At least, that's what the photographs say. Archana has not spoken to Sister Philomena in a long while, so she has no details. If she is to believe the pictures, her daughter is quite happy.

It's as though Fakii is reading her mind. 'You saw Janet recently and you know how the story with Prasad ended. What about your Shalini? You've been out of touch with her for so long. She'll be seeing you after fifteen years. Her life is very different now from when she was with you. Do you think she even remembers the last time you were together?'

Archana's mind flashes back to the last time she saw Shalu. That awful night. They had a huge fight over the cash. *'My God. I can't believe you are actually thinking of keeping the money. My parents? Their only daughter raped by three boys, and they are thinking of making money from it. I can't take this anymore.'*

Archana has replayed those words every day in her mind. What should they have done differently that night? Would it have changed anything? On the other hand, is Shalu alive because of that fight? Otherwise, she might have been asleep in her room.

Fakii knows exactly how that last conversation ended, with Shalini walking out on her parents.

'Do you think she still believes you were willing to settle for the cash, all those years ago? And that you killed her father?'

'No, she can't. I am in jail, am I not? How could she still think that?'

'Maybe she knows you were framed for the murder. But she doesn't know that you were not thinking about the money. What are you going to do to make her believe?'

'Are we back to talking revenge, Fakii?' Archana says, annoyed.

'Yes. But not for you. For Shalini. She needs to believe that her parents would do anything to right the wrongs done to her.'

'But what can I do? I've already spent so much time here. I've never done anything like this before. I don't want to get caught and end up back here.'

'Oh, stop moaning, Archana! Now listen to me. Firstly, I am sure all those involved have forgotten what happened so long ago. For them, it was just one more minor issue to deal with. No one is expecting anything to happen as a consequence of that, after all these years. So you have the element of surprise. Second, they are used to violence and know how to deal with violence. Therefore, you need to think of some other way. And third, you have time. You have two years to plan. Lastly, you have me. If I can help, I will. Just tell me and it will be done.'

Fakii stands up to leave. 'Now I have to go deal with some business. But think about what I said, ok?'

# 13

Archana lies back in bed thinking about all that Fakii said.

It's true, she has contemplated revenge often enough over the years. She was in shock when she was imprisoned for Raju's murder, but seeing Janet and hearing about Prasad's passing had shaken her. There are times when she wishes she could get a gun and shoot them all. It's become her favourite fantasy these last few weeks. But she knows that there is a whole system lined up against her and in favour of those in power. She doesn't stand a chance against it. All she can do, and has done, is make peace with prison time. Pay the price. She is not alone in this. So many people she has met in prison are here on false charges. They either did not know the law or were given the wrong advice or, most likely, were victims of bribes paid to judges or cops.

Then there are those like Fakii, who refuse to meekly accept the system and turn it to their advantage. What she said about Shalu wasn't far off the mark. Maybe Shalu does think that all those years ago, her parents were willing to settle for cash. Why did she and Raju not insist that Ajay take the suitcase away? Why did they let him leave it behind? If they had only acted sensibly then, none of this would have happened.

But who could have anticipated any of this? How naïve they were. They thought they would get Ajay to take the money away the next day and if he didn't, they would call the DGP and inform him that they were being bribed. So simple. So foolish.

God is meant to punish evil. But from what she can see, nothing seems to have happened to these evil people. Maybe God expects good people like her to fight against injustice and not just accept it. Didn't Fakii say something like that a few years ago? Something about her dharma being to fight back. At the time, she had dismissed the thought outright. But now, with Shalu foremost in her mind, she can't stop thinking about it.

These are vicious people. Look at what they did to Prasad. If she does act, with her limited capabilities, she will have to make sure nothing can be traced back to her. But what can she do? She has no money. No connections. She knows no one who can do anything to Nanjundaswamy and Palani. Except Fakii. And while she has offered, she doesn't want to be beholden to Fakii. Anyway, Fakii is in jail and has far more limited resources than Nanjundaswamy

But Fakii is right. She does have two years to plan her revenge. And she may be able to catch the enemy unawares. As far as they are concerned, the battle is long over, the war has been won. Mother in jail, father killed, daughter missing. What is there to worry about?

A few days later, while trying to fix a relatively new cell phone, the outline of a plan begins to form in Archana's mind. She tries to push it away, but it hovers on the edges of her imagination, demanding attention. Gradually, she lets it in, reshapes it, then tucks it away at the back of her mind till she can find the time to think through it. She knows that for someone with her skills, it shouldn't be a difficult thing to accomplish, but it will require a huge element of luck. Without that, it's impossible to even think of a scenario where one woman brings down an entire system of injustice. And what if she fails? They will destroy her.

Then, something happens to make up her mind.

Shortly after being made chief minister, Nanjundaswamy comes to Bangalore Central Jail for an inspection. Actually, more for a tour. Publicity. To show care and concern for the forgotten.

All the prisoners are ordered to clean up. Those who have recently got a change of clothes are told to stand in the yard when Nanjundaswamy arrives. He will walk past them, get a few photographs taken, have tea with the new superintendent.

As luck would have it, Archana is among the fifty women prisoners selected for Najundaswamy's reception. They stand in the open ground in front of the prison in one long line. Nanjundaswamy is to arrive at 10 a.m., but it's noon by the time he shows up. Accompanying him is Ajay.

The women stand, eyes downcast, motionless in the heat. There is a smell of stale sweat in the air, the stink of exhaustion after standing in the hot sun for hours.

Nanjundaswamy and Ajay stroll by, the former's cold gaze and smug smile indicative of his disdain for the women. They are the lowest of the low, after all.

As the two of them walk past with the superintendent, Ajay's eyes lock on to Archana's and almost instantly, recognition dawns. He steps over to Nanjundaswamy and whispers something in his ear. Nanjundaswamy stops and turns around, his eyes searching for Archana. He has never met her, so he needs Ajay to point her out to him. He stares at her for a while with a slimy smile and nods his head once. Then he turns and walks on.

It is only a moment for them, but in Archana it unleashes all the pent-up emotions she has tried so hard to suppress, the depth of misery this man has inflicted upon her. A blind, all-consuming rage rises within her. She knows that she cannot let him get away with it. She knows she has to act.

# Part III

# 1

Although the orders reach the jail in the morning, by the time the paperwork is done and she is allowed to leave, it is nearly 4 p.m. Exactly when it usually rains in Bangalore. And sure enough, when Archana steps out after fifteen years and two days, it is into a wet and windy city. She has a small bag with all her possessions and about fifty thousand rupees in cash, given to her as payment for the bits of work she did in prison.

Her farewell meeting with Fakii is short. 'Remember, don't wait for God to do something. Make your own destiny. And don't forget your sisters here. Inshallah, your daughter and you will be united soon.'

Whatever else may have changed in the city over the years, its inability to deal with rain remains unchanged. Archana finds herself in ankle-deep water as soon as she steps outside the gate. Tentatively, she takes a few steps forward, letting the rain soak into her clothes and wash away the stench of the prison. Her hair is plastered to her head, wet tendrils cling to her forehead and shoulders. She lifts her face up to the sky, invigorated by the cold water drizzling down on her face.

She walks a few hundred metres along a desolate, tree-lined street towards the main road. A passing car stops to take a picture of a fifty-five-year-old woman laughing as she faces the rain open-mouthed. Everywhere she looks, people are taking shelter to avoid the rain. She walks on purposefully for a few minutes before she spots a small tea stall and sits down on the bench in front. She asks for a hot cup of tea with sugar and milk. The way she likes it, not the way the jail wanted her to have it.

She turns to the old man next to her and asks in Kannada, 'Sir, can I make one call from your phone?' The man turns to her, and seeing a haggard, yellow-toothed woman, picks up his cup and steps away.

As she looks away disappointed, a young man, probably in his early thirties, sits down beside her and offers her his phone. Seeing her surprised look, he says in a mixture of Tamil and Kannada, 'Amma, my mother is your age, and I hope that someday, if she needs a phone, someone will offer it to her. Here, please use it.'

Archana looks at the man. Thick black hair parted on the side, a small saffron band around his head. Tattoos across both muscular arms in the Tamil script. A sacred thread is tied around his left wrist and a gold chain around his neck. Nothing in his look suggests kindness.

'Thank you, maga. Your mother has brought you up well. I pray that she always gets the help that she needs, whenever she needs. I just need to make one call,' she adds.

'No problem.'

Archana smiles at him in gratitude. From memory she dials a number she has not dialled for fifteen years. The phone rings twice before someone picks up.

'Hello?' says the voice on the phone.

Archana tries to compose herself but fails. In a shaky voice, she says, 'Janet?'

'Archana? Sorry, sorry. I am on the way. The traffic in this rain, you know how it is, becomes worse every year. Fifteen minutes max. Just turned in from Hosur road. Can't wait to see you, Archu. Hang in there!'

'Don't worry. They told me you had been informed. I am just outside the jail, in a small tea shop just up the road. It's the only one here.'

'Yes, yes. Coming!'

Archana hangs up. She looks around her and the loneliness hits like a tsunami. What is she going to do for the rest of her life? How will she cope?

'Amma, would you like something to eat?'

Archana looks up to see the same young man standing in front of her, watching her kindly. She shakes her head. 'No. You've been kind enough to me. If you had not shown up, I don't know what I would have done. Thank you. Here, take your phone. It was a local call. You can check.'

'No, Amma. It's fine. Hope your sad days end today with the rains and you find happiness. Take care.' The young man gets on his motorcycle, dons his helmet and rides off in the light drizzle.

Archana orders another cup of tea and thinks of the simple, daily pleasures that people outside prison take for granted. They are just going about their business without anyone watching them, escorting them, beating them.

Thirty minutes later, a small grey car draws up to the tea shop and a woman with short, grey hair gets out, her eyes searching for a familiar face. Archana slowly stands up and takes a few steps towards the car. Janet sees her and runs to her, pulls her into her arms wordlessly. The two women weep unabashedly amidst the strangers standing nearby.

'Finally. You're out. The nightmare is over. You're free. I can't believe it.'

Janet opens the passenger door and gently helps Archana into the car. Then she gets back behind the steering wheel and drives them both home.

The two old friends talk non-stop as the car inches along through the worsening traffic, past two-wheelers and large SUVs that behave like they own the road. Archana learns that Prasad's insurance money has come through and Janet has bought the small apartment in JP Nagar that Archana had visited on furlough. She has also started a small digital content marketing agency. A combination of hard work and some luck has helped the business grow and she is in a good place now.

2

Janet leads Archana to the guest bedroom that has been done up for her. A set of new clothes has been laid out on the bed along with her favourite perfume. The room is fragrant with the smell of tuberoses that stand in a vase on the bedside table. On the dressing table is a framed photograph of Raju, Shalini and Archana from when Shalu was just a little baby. Archana picks up the photo and looks at it, letting the memories of that day in Cubbon Park wash over her.

'Rest, have a bath, whatever you want to do, Archu. I'll be sitting right outside, in the living room.'

Archana sits on the edge of the soft bed and feels herself sink into it. She lies back slowly, her weary body taking a moment to recall what a good mattress feels like.

An hour later, Archana wakes up with a start. She can't remember the last time she slept so deeply. She quickly opens the door to her room and looks out to see Janet scrolling through photographs on her phone, her cheeks wet with tears. Hearing Archana, she looks up and holds her arms out. The two of them sit quietly beside each other, holding hands, each lost in her thoughts.

'I am sorry, Janet, I didn't mean to fall asleep,' Archana says quietly.

'It's all right, Archu. No hurry. We have nothing planned for the day. I am going to order in some dinner. I also have some wine chilling.

Only one glass for you today. Tomorrow, maybe two. Then we'll see,' Janet says, laughing.

Archana returns in half an hour wearing clean, crisply ironed clothes. It's a novel feeling. Janet pours two glasses of white wine and the women sits across from each other in the sparsely furnished living room. Archana looks around. Janet's old house in Malleshwaram was so different. The expensive paintings, the fancy furniture, the lamps, all gone now. This is an anonymous two-bedroom flat. A small living room with three single-seater sofas, a centre table on which are scattered some books and the day's newspaper. On the wall is a photograph of Prasad and Janet in happier times on a boat somewhere.

'Janet, I know I said I would like to stay here for a few days, but it may take some time for me to find my feet and decide what to do next,' Archana says.

'Archu, don't talk rubbish. You are staying here till you get your own place. If you want to, you can stay here forever. I have no visitors, ever. But if you want to move, you can do so whenever you are ready. My only condition is that you have to be in this same building. That's non-negotiable. I've also decided that you'll join my business as a cofounder.'

'What? Don't be silly. I don't know anything about content. What use can I be to you?'

'Archu, I am being very selfish. The future is all about mobile phones and already, nearly all the content we are creating is for the phone. I don't know very much about mobile technology, but I do know that you were working with it all those years ago. It won't take you long to get up to speed with the new technologies. Then you and I can take on the world. Trust me, I am not doing this as charity. I really could use you. Try it for six months, and if you don't like it, I'll help you find something you like. Deal?'

Her friend sounds so enthusiastic, Archana gives in without hesitation. Not that she has many options.

'And, of course, we need to go bring Shalu home. Now that are out, it's time for the great reunion.'

'Oh, you don't know how much I want to. But I think we should take it slow. She must still be mad at me. For killing her father. That's what the courts found, right? And that's what all the newspapers reported as well. She doesn't know the truth, and even if I tell her, why will she believe me? I need to figure out a way to get her to trust me again. And that will take some time.'

'People say all kinds of things when they are angry, Archu. I am sure she has had enough time to cool down.'

'Maybe, but I don't want to take the chance of losing her again. I need to make sure she knows what happened and that she forgives her parents.'

'And how do you plan to do that, Archu?'

'I have a plan brewing, but the less you know the better.'

'Is dinner here yet? I am really hungry,' she says before Janet can probe any further. 'And by the way, when we go out tomorrow, I need to buy a laptop and a phone. I think I need a six-month salary advance!'

'Founders don't get salaries. They only get stock options,' replies Janet laughingly.

For a moment, it feels like their troubles are in the past and normalcy is within reach.

3

Archana quickly settles down to a routine. She gets up early, goes for a walk around the huge apartment complex. By seven, Janet is awake and the two of them have tea while catching up on the world news. Janet gets her updates on the phone;

Archana reads the day's newspapers. At around nine, the two of them drive off to work together.

After her initial discomfort at sitting behind a computer and meeting people, Archana's old confidence returns. She is able to hold her own in discussions about technology and mobile phone usage. Her time in prison has given her a unique insight into people's phone behaviour. She quickly becomes an office favourite because she is always willing to help with any task that needs doing. The art of listening, learnt and practised in prison, has become an asset.

Archana contacts Sister Philomena to inform her that she is out of prison but not ready to meet Shalu just yet. Now it is she who needs to feel strong enough to meet her daughter. She shares her new number with Sister Philomena so that she can continue to get photographs and updates of her grown-up daughter.

She is scrolling through old photographs on her phone, taking time off from trying to solve a complex UX problem, when there is a knock on the door. It's Janet.

Archana raises an eyebrow at her.

'I have a surprise visitor for you, Archu,' Janet says, stepping aside so Archana can see the visitor.

It's a familiar face, although older. With a lot more grey in the hair, but the same friendly smile. 'SI Varma?' Archana smiles back in return.

'I was not aware of your early release. I didn't have any contact details for you either. I took a chance that you would be here. So good to see you outside and free, Mrs Gowda. I know many years of life have been lost, but you still have many years ahead of you.

'Also, I am not SI anymore. I am now DGP for Karnataka. I am back in Bangalore, since the last two months.'

'Congratulations, DGP Varma. That is very good news. I am so happy that you are back in Bangalore,' Archana says with a broad smile. In the next moment, she remembers. 'But how is it, having that man as CM?' she asks.

'Mrs Gowda, we have to learn to adjust. All jobs in the government service are like this now. Politics is in everything. We try to do the best we can, within our constraints.'

'DGP—'

'Madam, you can call me Varma.'

'Ok then, Varma. What brings you here? Keeping an eye on old criminals?' Archana asks with a twinkle in her eye.

'Oh no, Mrs Gowda. When I heard you were released, I had to come and see you. Check if you are ok and if I can help in any way.'

'You are very kind, Varma. But I am all right.' She looks at him silently for a moment, then something compels her to confess, 'There's still a big hole in my heart, Varma. I have to find the courage to meet Shalini. And life without Raju, outside the jail ... it's very hard.'

'How is she? Your daughter. Have you been to meet her?'

'No, no. I still haven't gone to meet her. I'm not ready to face her, Varma. The time will come, soon. But I am happy that she is doing well. Sister Philomena sends me photographs and updates. Shalini is now the vice principal of a school in Coonoor. She lives in a small house very close to the school.'

After a cup of tea and some more pleasantries, Varma departs, leaving Archana with her thoughts. And a niggling worry: with Varma back in the city, her plan will have to be watertight. But it's a chance she has to take. For her Shalu.

## 4

First thing in the morning, Archana opens her laptop and creates a secure folder. Then she makes a list of the people she has to deal with.

There is Thomas. The boy who allowed Shalu to go with Palani.

The two brothers, Ahmed and Samir, who participated in the crime.

Palani, the primary culprit.

Ajay, the man who set them up.

Najundaswamy, the puppet master.

And the DGP. The man who made sure the plan succeeded.

As she looks at the list of seven names, a shudder runs through her. She has never even shouted at Shalu, and here she is, planning revenge against so many people, including the chief minister of the state. It sounds absurd, even to her. But thanks to Fakii, she does not lack the courage.

She says a silent prayer and settles down to her task. First, she must track each of the men and find out what they are up to. She creates a few fake accounts on social media—LinkedIn, Facebook and Instagram. In disguise, she tracks down the four boys, now men. Thomas, Ahmed, Samir and Palani. Where they are, what they do. Their marriages, relationships, family life, holiday destinations, favourite movies and food are all laid out for everyone to see. It is amazing what social media has enabled. For a coder like her, it is a moment's work to access their phone numbers and locate each of their devices. Fortunately, they are all in Bangalore.

Chief Minister Nanjundaswamy is a little harder to track. She hacks into the mobile phone tower near the CM's house in the Golf Course area and starts tracking the phones that are active in the vicinity. At any point in time, there are hundreds of phones. Residents, visitors, security staff, support staff and so on. She gives each of the devices a number and maps their time in the area, as well as when they come and go. Separately, she tracks Nanjundaswamy's travels around the city and the state. Over a period of one week, she identifies a few phones that spend the most time in the network or are mapped to Nanjundaswamy's travels. One or two of them are sure to be his. Another couple are probably Ajay's. The one that remains for the longest time in his house is likely to be that of his wife. Remotely, she switches on the phone mics to help tag each phone to the correct person. In a few hours she is able to identify Nanjundaswamy's two phones, Ajay's two, and the one belonging to his wife. Which means she now has eyes on two more of the people on her list.

Tracking ex-IG Bhaskar's phone turns out to be more difficult because she does not know where he stays. But she does have DGP Varma's phone number. She gets into Varma's phone and, using his contact list, gets Bhaskar's number. And through that she is able to identify the location of the device and where he lives.

The first phase of her plan is done. All seven people have been tracked down. Now she moves to phase two.

Phase two is about listening in, trying to understand the life and routine of each person, and thinking through opportunities to exact revenge.

While she can get in and out of their phones without being traced, she is aware of the risk of Varma or Janet joining the dots if something happens too quickly to these seven people who are united only by the one crime. It's important to move slowly and not do anything too obvious.

More than fifteen years have passed since that awful day. A few months more will not make a difference. Archana tells herself to be patient.

5

The first person she decides to deal with is Thomas.

In many ways, he is the one who is responsible for what happened to Shalu. He was her friend. He had been to their house so many times.

Archana knew his parents. Shalu trusted him enough that when he offered to drop her home, she agreed immediately. And he just handed her over to Palani. Surely he would have known of Palani's reputation. He should have got an auto or asked Shalu to call her father. He didn't. And then he stood watch outside the car when the brutes were assaulting her daughter.

Archana begins an intense online scan of Thomas's life. She finds out that he did exceedingly well in school and went to the US for higher studies. He graduated from an Ivy league college, studied for an MBA, then joined a top Venture Capital firm. He worked in the US for five years and returned to India as a managing director for one of the major VCs in the country.

He has been married and divorced. He now lives alone in one of the poshest apartment complexes in central Bangalore. He bought the flat a few months ago. From what Archana can make out, it's one of those smart homes. Google smart. Things that run on voice commands, things that happen automatically or in response to pre-programmed instructions. High security, with CCTV cameras. No one can get in or out without prior invitation and photographs being taken. Not that Archana has any desire to get anywhere close to Thomas. But she needs to get close enough to know more about his life.

She repeats the same hack that she used to allow the old superintendent to see his daughter's messages. She calls Thomas. When he answers, she pretends to be someone selling insurance. He cuts her off rudely. But that's enough for her to sneak her way into his phone and scan all his messages, calls, photographs and apps.

Thomas clearly lives a very fancy life. His phone is full of photographs of him at workshops, vacations in expensive-looking hotels, on yachts and beaches. He looks a lot like he did in his teens. A thick bushy moustache and rimless glasses are the new add-ons. And his fancy clothes. When Archana knew him, he was a simple boy living with his parents. His father worked for one of the oil companies. Indian Oil, she thinks. Clearly, he has done pretty well for himself.

The apps on his phone are the usual ones: cab services, social media, financial services, security, and some games. Just like a normal person. At first, she thinks she should just clean out his bank account or dupe him in some online scam. But that would not be adequate punishment. He might get his money back, claiming an error. That's not good enough. She needs to look harder.

Then she finds it. Or, at least, something she can try.

A thermostat app controls the temperature in his apartment. It works with preset recommended limits of course, but if she can control the setting and make sure Thomas cannot change it at his end, she may be able to pull off something drastic.

Archana sets up a non-stop vigil through her laptop on Thomas's activities, searching for the right moment to pounce. His weekdays are quite predictable, with office in the daytime and work calls in the evening. The weekends are when he goes wild. Lots of parties. Late nights. Occasionally, he brings a girl home. But on most nights he returns alone, very drunk, and sleeps late into the next day.

And so it happens, one Friday night, or rather, Saturday morning. Thomas comes home completely drunk. It's nearly 4 a.m. He barely makes it to his bed before passing out. In seconds, he is dead to the world.

'Ok, my boy. Let's see if you can get out of this,' Archana mutters to herself as she logs into his phone app. She sets the thermostat to its lowest temperature of 10 degrees Celsius. Then she enables the smart locks of the bedroom door and the windows, which are pre-set to only respond to his voice or his fingerprints. If her plan works, the cold will render Thomas's voice too dry and different to be recognised by the system. The same with his fingers, making it hard for him to activate his phone. But more importantly, by the time he registers that it's too cold, his body would have become too weak to act.

To ensure that he does not call anyone for help, she disables his mobile network and the Wi-Fi on the phone by activating the airplane mode. From all that she has read about medical conditions, she figures that Thomas's heart will start giving way in a couple of hours, and in another hour it will all be over.

She is a bundle of nerves. If Raju were here, he would be shocked. On the other hand, if Raju were here, she wouldn't be doing any of the things she plans to do over the coming weeks. Thomas deserves it. They all deserve what is coming their way.

It is nearly 5 a.m. by the time Archana is done with executing her plan, and she will not know if it has worked till about mid-morning the next day. She is too wired to sleep, so she puts on her shoes to go for a walk. When she comes out of her room, Janet is already sitting in the living room, gazing out the French doors.

'What's the matter, Janet?' Archana asks, hurrying to her side.

'Some days I miss Prasad so much, Archu. I can't sleep. I just lie awake all night.' Tears well up in her eyes as she speaks.

'Oh, my dear. I am so sorry. I understand. It's been sixteen years for me and I still wake up some nights looking for Raju next to me. It's happening less often these days, but it does. I don't think we'll ever get over our loss.'

Janet shakes her head sadly and sits still for a few minutes.

'By the way, what's going on with you, Archu? You look busier than usual these days. Is everything ok?' she asks, looking at Archana searchingly.

'Oh, yes. All is fine. Doing some skill share programmes to speed up my tech-savviness outside of mobile phones. All this content stuff you've got me doing doesn't leave me with much time to update my skills.' Archana laughs to hide her consternation.

'I am going for my walk. Want to come?'

'Yes, let me put on my shoes. One minute.'

At about 11 a.m., Archana uses her laptop to get into Thomas's phone again. She turns on the phone network and Wi-Fi. She switches on his mic, but there is silence on the other side. She gets back into the thermostat app and brings the temperature back to a more normal 22 degrees.

Removes all traces of her having been in Thomas's phone and logs off.

Now to wait for developments.

## 6

### Tragic Loss for Venture Capitalists fraternity

The business world is mourning the sudden and untimely passing of Thomas Chacko, managing director of Nestaway Venture Funds. The prominent venture capitalist was found lifeless in the doorway of his high-end apartment yesterday morning.

Initial reports from law enforcement place the cause of death as a heart attack that led to organ failure. Just one night prior, Mr Chacko was seen celebrating a friend's engagement at Malibu, Bangalore's most popular nightclub. Witnesses said he seemed healthy and in good spirits as he exited the venue and left in a taxi.

The police will only issue an official statement after the post-mortem.

Mr Chacko is survived by his parents and his ex-wife.

## 7

'Archu, Archu, did you see this?' Janet comes running into Archana's room, waving a newspaper. 'Isn't he the guy who …'

'Let me see.'

Archana reads the short piece in silence, absorbing the news of her first murder. Murder. She has actually killed someone. Technically, she has got someone killed, but that's not how the law will see it. Will God ever forgive her?

But He is the one who put her in this position in the first place. If He were kinder, all these people would get their punishment directly. Instead, she has to intervene.

'Hello? Where have you got lost?'

'Yes, he is one of those boys. I thought I knew him well and trusted Shalu with him. How wrong I was. I think he deserved to die a more painful death than this. But I am glad he's gone.'

'Yes. God calling back the evil ones,' says Janet. 'This calls for a celebration. Cake for breakfast!'

'Sounds good, Janet.' At the back of Archana's mind is a nagging worry about the post-mortem. Will the police find something?

As if on cue, her phone rings. She freezes. It's DGP Varma. Why is he calling her? Have they found something already? They couldn't have. She has been so careful. But she is no expert in these things. It is her first time. Maybe she has made some basic errors.

She takes a deep breath and tries to sound calm. 'Good morning, Varma. How come so early in the morning?'

'Good morning, madam. Did you read the news about Thomas Chacko? I am sure you remember him.'

'Yes, Varma. It's not likely that I would forget him. Janet just showed me the news. I cannot say I am sad. Heart attack, huh? He was only about thirty years old, no?'

'Thirty-two. He seems to have led a very stressful life, so perhaps such a death is not unexpected.'

'The papers say something about a post-mortem. Is that normal?' Archana probes.

'Usually we do it only if there's something we hope to find out. The preliminary finding in this case is a heart attack. We found him in his bedroom, right next to the door. It looks like he was trying to get out. We think that when he had his heart attack, he tried to reach out to someone. His phone was in his hand, but broken. So maybe, when he got out of bed, the phone fell from his hand. Then he tried to get up, but died before he could. The post-mortem will help us confirm the sequence of events. If the family wants to file a suit against the smart lock company, they will use the findings of the post-mortem. Not that we expect to find anything unexpected, but we still need to reconfirm. That's all.'

'Oh, I see.'

'Mrs Gowda, I understand how you feel. The man who put Shalini in the position she finds herself in today was surely a monster. I don't know if you know this, but he did show great remorse later in life. He donated lakhs of rupees to charities that support young girls and women. Besides, he was the only son to his parents. And the father has Parkinson's. A heartbreaking loss for them, no doubt.'

'I can neither forgive nor forget what he did all those years ago,' Archana says fiercely, her hands tightening around the phone. 'He escaped your laws, Varma, but he deserved what he got!'

She hangs up, the tension draining out of her gradually. Will her own heart hold out, she wonders. She has pulled this one off, but there are six more to go.

## 8

A few days later, Archana moves into a rented apartment two floors below Janet's. They are both happy with this arrangement. Archana is glad to have her own space and privacy. Not that either woman has any sort of social life, or friends to hang out with. They spend all their spare time together. They go shopping, eat out, watch movies. But mostly they sit together, lost in their own thoughts, thinking of the lives lost and the lives that could have been lived.

Janet has extracted a promise from Archana that she will come over for dinner every night. After a long day at work, this arrangement suits her well. They also continue to commute to work together.

Archana waits a few weeks for things to settle down after Thomas's death. But she spends a lot of time following the developments, especially with regard to the post-mortem. As far as she can tell from the news, no new evidence has been found and the death, it has been decided, was from natural causes.

Now it's time to focus on the next target. Samir and Ahmed.

Online research reveals that the two brothers have joined their family business. The father started as a real-estate broker and then moved on to property development. His two sons were not very good at academics and seemed happy to float about. So he pulled them into the business. Samir, the elder boy, seems content with keeping his father's business going. Ahmed is more ambitious. But he is headstrong and doesn't spend much time thinking about the consequences of his actions or their long-term impact. It is to keep him out of his hair that his father appears to have agreed to Ahmed's plan of getting into garments. They set up a store on Commercial Street and invested in a garment factory in Bommasandra. It cost a lot of money, but the initial results were promising.

Money is always tight due to Ahmed's spendthrift ways. He has just gone and bought himself a new Audi SUV. It's the kind of money they do not want to spend, but no one can argue with Ahmed about anything. He uses his fists instead of words.

Not that Samir is a paragon of virtue. It's just that, compared to Ahmed, he seems more mature.

Unlike Thomas, who seemed to have changed his ways or at least did not repeat his crime, these two brothers have fought with everyone in their neighbourhood. And with each other. Especially with each other. Even now they are not averse to getting physical with each other. Their father often has to intervene to separate them.

Their friendship with Palani, however, has stayed strong over the years. They are very alike in so many ways. Prone to violence. Unafraid of the law. Operating under the code of 'anything goes'. Additionally, real estate and retail are good cover for any money laundering that Palani or his father wish to do. The three of them meet often to discuss ongoing deals and a new land scam that they hope will net them a few crores.

On the business front, the last few years have been pretty rough. High interest rates mean that the number of people investing in property has declined. Thanks to the pandemic, people are going out less, shopping less. There is labour trouble in their factory. Ahmed has resorted to violence, as is his wont, and it has backfired. The staff have locked up the factory and gone on strike.

By now, Archana has spent hours looking at their photographs and reading about them. If only she could see them up close. It's a bold move for her, but this is not the old Archana anymore. First, she travels to Commercial Street and visits the garment store under the pretext of buying fabric. As she pretends to look for some cloth to make shirts, she looks around and spots Ahmed sitting behind the cash counter in the corner. He has a thick beard and a prematurely thinning head of black hair. Bushy eyebrows, and what looks like a permanent scowl. He is busy on his phone. At one point, he lifts his head and looks at Archana. She freezes. But he has never seen her, and anyway, even those who knew her before she went to jail would struggle to recognise her now. He returns his gaze to the phone, ignoring her and the rest of the people in the store. Archana is sure the salesperson across from her can hear her heart racing. She feels a wave of panic and quickly leaves the store without buying anything.

She doesn't think she can go through this again, but for Shalu she has to. After all, Shalu saw these faces up close. Archana needs to see them as well. Look into their malignant eyes once, before she deals with them.

The next day, she drives down to their real-estate office on Wheeler Road. From the data she has accessed, she knows that Samir is usually in the office in the afternoon, while Ahmed is at the store. Ahmed arrives after 5 p.m. and the brothers talk business. And fight.

Archana parks her car and finds a window seat at a Third Wave Coffee outlet from where she has a direct view into Samir's office. There's only a young boy there. A little later, a well-built man of medium height, wearing a blue shirt and jeans, arrives. He has a beard and a full head of hair. This has to be Samir. He says something to the boy, who runs out immediately. Samir turns on his computer and pulls out his phone, in which he is soon engrossed. Ten minutes later, he sits down and gets busy on the computer. Thanks to the glass front, Archana has a clear view of him.

Now that she has read all she could find online about them and seen their faces, she can tell herself that, unlike Thomas, there is nothing redeeming about these two.

A few days later, she sends a message to Samir. All it says is, 'Checked your bank account recently?' Below it is a link to their corporate account website. That's it.

Curious, Samir logs into the bank account and finds that it is down to a few thousand rupees. He is shocked. Just last evening he had managed to bring in two crore rupees by borrowing from some people in his network from whom he would have preferred to stay well away. He checks the previous transactions and finds that Ahmed has transferred the entire amount to his personal account.

Samir loses it. He barges into Ahmed's room.

'How dare you take the money without talking to me? It's for the business,' he shouts.

'I have no idea what you are talking about. Now leave. I am in the midst of something,' Ahmed replies haughtily.

'You can't just take all the money I brought in,' Samir insists.

'I'm telling you again. I don't know what you are talking about. Just get out now. Or there'll be trouble.'

'Trouble? Really? You don't know trouble. Did you take the money to buy another car? Or give your useless wife another present? I don't care, the money better come back into the account in fifteen minutes!'

'Who are you calling useless? You think you can get away with that?' Ahmed pushes his chair back and leans forward threateningly.

Samir looks him in the eye and says, 'Yes, useless. Your wife is useless. You are useless. The whole lot of you are useless. Anyway, I don't care about that. I want the money back, and now!'

'Screw the money,' Ahmed hisses. He jumps up and punches Samir in the face.

Samir staggers back, puts his hand to his nose, sees the blood gushing out, and rushes towards Ahmed. The two men go at each other. Slaps, kicks. They are on the floor, on the table, bouncing off the walls. Bloody noses, torn shirts, ripped pants, and yet they don't stop.

It is then that Samir pulls out a gun to get Ahmed to stop fighting. But Ahmed does not stop. He charges Samir, grabbing his gun hand and wrestling him for the weapon. A moment later, the gun goes off. Both men freeze, shocked out of their wits. Then Samir looks down and sees the blood seeping out of his stomach. Within seconds he collapses on the floor, moaning with pain. A minute or so after that, he is dead.

Ahmed is stunned. Hearing the gunshot, people have started gathering outside the office. They see Ahmed still holding the smoking gun. He looks from his dead brother to the gun to the crowd outside. He has no choice. Waving the gun, he runs out of the building, gets into his car and speeds away.

Sometime later, the police are on the scene. As they cordon off the crime scene and seal the office, Archana remotely deletes the last message sent to Samir's phone.

## 9

# SHOOT OUT ENDS IN DOUBLE TRAGEDY

Yesterday afternoon, in a shooting incident in Cox Town, one person was shot dead. Samir and Ahmed Ansari, two brothers running a real-estate business, got engaged in an argument over some business matters. As the argument escalated into a physical fight, a gunshot was heard, resulting in the death of Samir Ansari. Ahmed Ansari, who is the alleged shooter, escaped in his SUV. After a prolonged search, police found Ahmed Ansari's body near the railway tracks behind Windsor Manor. Preliminary investigations reveal that he took his own life by jumping in front of a passing train.

Neighbours of the Ansari brothers say that the two men had a history of troublemaking and had made life difficult for people living on the street with their constant fights and acts of violence. It is understood that their business has been facing tough times due to the pandemic and their factory's closure.

The two men are survived by their wives and father.

# 10

Archana puts the paper down. Her hands are trembling and her legs can barely support her. Both brothers dealt with in one shot. This is more than she hoped for. Besides, there's no mention in the paper about it being anything more than a fight gone wrong. Can it be that something was left out of the news? She knows that sometimes the police don't release all the information that they have.

She has done nothing more than arrange for the money to move from the business account to Ahmed's personal account and send that message to Samir. But still, she needs to know.

She dials a number she knows by heart.

'Good morning, Varma, I hope I am not disturbing you,' she says.

'Good morning, madam. No, I have fifteen minutes before going to drop my son to the bus stop. What can I do for you?' he asks.

'I just saw the news about the Ansaris. Are these the same two who … ?'

'Yes, madam,' he replies immediately. 'The same. I have to say, though it is a loss of two human lives, no one will mourn their passing. They were just very troublesome people.'

'Oh, I see. It looks like one brother shot the other and then took his own life. Is that so?' she asks, trying to conceal her anxiety and get what she can out of him.

'Yes, Mrs Gowda. Seems pretty simple. There are enough eyewitnesses to the fight, the shooting, the escape, and even the suicide,' he says.

Archana breathes a sigh of relief. 'And this time you are not going to tell me that they were amazing do-gooders, are you?'

DGP Varma laughs out loud.

'Oh no, madam. These two were bad through and through. I hear that even their father had a tough time managing them. As far as the police are concerned, it's good when people like these are finished without our help. Otherwise, we have to catch them, do lots of paperwork, and then some smart lawyer will get them off. This way is clean and we can all thank God.'

'Everyone wins, except the bad men,' Archana says with a laugh. 'I'll let you go now. My regards to your family.'

She puts the phone down, a broad smile on her face. Her plan may still work. With the Ansaris she had to rely on the inherent suspicion between the brothers and wasn't really in a position to plan the outcome. Eventually, though, it turned out well.

Three down. Four to go.

## 11

She is getting close to the head of the snake. She knows she needs to be patient. And very careful. Thomas and the two brothers were relatively easy to deal with. They were so entirely unsuspecting. Nanjundaswamy, Palani and Ajay, on the other hand, are unreachable. Their guard is always up. Anything out of the ordinary and they would set their people on it, with brutal consequences.

Fakii once compared Nanjundaswamy to a wounded tiger. Whatever plan Archana comes up with, she knows it can only have one result—she must destroy him completely. There is no doubt in her mind that he deserves it. Both Raju and Prasad are gone because of him. Janet is a shell of her former shelf. And Shalu—there is always the matter of Shalu, with whom it all began.

Like with the Ansari brothers, she spends time understanding how Nanjundaswamy and Palani live and think. YouTube is awash with videos of Nanjundaswamy making speeches and being interviewed by various journalists. He has a set template, which includes making big promises about a bright, golden future and blaming previous chief ministers for the current state of affairs. Never mind that his party has been running Karnataka for over twelve years now.

Archana wonders how someone like him has managed to win elections and become chief minister. Clearly, it's easy to fool most of the people at least some of the time. In one interview, he is asked about law and order and he replies looking directly at the camera, 'No matter the crime, no matter the criminal, my orders to the police are clear. Spare no one.' To Archana it feels like he is talking directly to her.

She starts her twenty-four-hour vigil, tracking the phones of Nanjundaswamy, Palani and Ajay. The microphones are activated and connected to her laptop where everything gets recorded. Archana listens to it all, then deletes it. Anything important or useful is transcribed into a document in one of her hidden folders.

When she first gets into Nanjundaswamy's phone, she is stunned. It's like entering a whole other world of chaos. There's lots of information, most of it meaningless and continually changing. There's a Telegram group that focuses on the inflow and outflow of cash with cryptic mentions of +5 RK, –3 DV, +8 AG and so on. It takes a while for Archana to figure out that the numbers are rupees in crores, the + and – mean the amount is being credited or debited, respectively, and the initials refer to the names of various people.

There is a separate group that has details of where the money lies and how much there is. Ajay is a part of this group, and every morning he briefs Nanjundaswamy on the total amount in each location and what is expected that day. It's like running a large cash business, Archana thinks.

She looks through the folder of photographs on Nanjundaswamy's phone and finds inside it another, hidden folder containing hundreds of incriminating photographs of politicians and celebrities caught in less than flattering circumstances. Many of them can be explained away as innocent moments, but if they get into the media, the dirt would stick. Clearly, Nanjundaswamy has no qualms about trading them in for favours for himself or his team. That would explain some of the cash coming in.

And then she sees the photograph. Of a smiling, innocent Shalu from a social media post before her hell began. Archana looks at it, shocked, unable to make sense of its presence here in Nanjundaswamy's phone. Then, without even stopping to think, she copies the image and immediately deletes it from the folder. Shalini needs to be with her mother, not with the chief minister.

## 12

Over the next few weeks, Archana painstakingly puts together a detailed profile of Nanjundaswamy. He appears to have devoted his life to politics; family comes a distant second. His wife, seven years younger than him, is happy to remain in the background. A qualified doctor who practised medicine before marriage, she is now content to while away her time doing up the many houses that her husband owns. She meets a small group of old school friends once a week for lunch, sometimes for a drink. Stories about home and family are exchanged. Some days they play cards or go shopping together. Archana realises from the conversations she overhears that the chief minister's wife finds the atmosphere at home suffocating. Given that the job of a politician never ends, there is always someone to meet him every hour of the day and night. So she has begun to confine herself to a couple of rooms at the back of the house.

Nanjundaswamy has great hopes that Palani will follow him into politics. But he doesn't seem to want to do anything at all. He is supposed to manage the family's real-estate business, but he appears to be unable to get anything done without getting into trouble. And that causes frequent flare-ups between father and son.

Like the one this morning, which Archana eavesdrops on.

'Palani, what's the issue with the Hennur Road property?' Nanjundaswamy asks in Tulu.

'There's no issue,' replies Palani, his voice sullen.

'Then why did I get a call about it?'

'Ajay and his big mouth! I don't know why they come to you for everything.'

'Well, it is our property and I am the chief minister. If anything happens that could make life difficult for me, I need to know well in advance so that we can manage it. That is Ajay's job.'

'I don't know why you say it's my responsibility if, between Ajay and you, you manage everything,' replies Palani. There is the sound of a chair being scraped back.

'You fool! You *are* responsible. Responsible for everything that goes wrong. What made you go after that tax inspector? He was just doing his job. You could have called Ajay, he would have spoken to someone and the fellow would have backed off. But no. You had to get him beaten up. Now he's in hospital and the police are asking questions. An immature idiot, that's what you are.'

'If that's the way you feel, then just give it all to Ajay to manage. Why pull me into it?' Palani sounds sulky.

There is silence for a moment. Then Nanjundaswamy's voice comes through loud and clear.

'It is our property. I want you to learn how to handle it. It's going to be yours sooner or later.'

'Either you let me do it my way or you do it. I don't like this backseat driving. If you want it done your way, then I won't do it. Give me something else to do.'

'Do this first. Do it well. Show me that you can do something after all. Then I'll see what else to give you. Right now, you are just a good-for-nothing fellow coasting on my reputation.'

'Poppa …'

'Don't Poppa me,' Nanjundaswamy snaps. 'Go with Ajay to the hospital. Meet that tax inspector. Find a way to stop him from filing a case. Don't beat him up, for God's sake. Cajole him out of it. If you can't, let Ajay handle it. I want this case to go away. Elections are coming up in a few months and I don't want to give the opposition any opportunity to make a noise.'

Over the next few days, Archana is often shocked by the conversations she overhears, the things Nanjundaswamy asks to get done. Bribing or threatening people like the tax inspector seems to be a regular affair. Breaking someone's legs and beating up people come naturally to him. If he doesn't get things the easy way, he is happy for blood to be spilt.

The only people he seems to tiptoe around are two of the national party leaders. They appear to be as ruthless as he is and happy to sacrifice anyone at all for the sake of the party. Nanjundaswamy expresses appropriate servitude, though he disses them in private. He knows his survival depends entirely on them and he can never aspire to their jobs. He has reached as high as he can in the party. Now all his skills are put to use to ensure he stays in the chief minister's seat for as long as possible.

And that's where she decides to hit him. If he is unmasked as an opportunist who is disloyal to his own party, it could end his career. No one will touch him. And without his politics, he is nothing.

# 13

Archana is ready. It's all coming to a head, and she will either succeed or be back in jail, or worse: she will become a victim of Nanjundaswamy's goons, yet again. But she cannot stop now.

At exactly 9 p.m. on a rainy Friday night, from a spoofed account, she drops four audio recordings on a few social media channels, tagging multiple journalists and some news channels. The first recording features Nanjundaswamy talking about his political leaders in Delhi in extremely disparaging terms. In very uncouth language, he talks about how the national leadership is ineffective and the party is entirely dependent on him and his political skills to succeed in the state.

In the second recording, he is speaking of a recent by-election that his party has won. He is gloating about voters being gullible enough to believe all his campaign promises, especially the one about the gift of 200 units of free power for everyone. The third recording contains hints that a politician who is widely considered to be his successor will never make it because Nanjundaswamy himself will block his path with assistance from his political camp. The last recording is, relatively speaking, the least harmless. In it he asks the Municipal Commissioner to find a way to grant a mega tunnel project to a shell company in which he and Palani have a major stake.

The release of the recordings causes a stir. Every network telecasts them in an endless loop. Party spokesmen turn up on every channel to defend the chief minister. Nanjundaswamy and his confidants, including Ajay, form a crisis team to try and salvage the situation; they suggest that his voice has been manipulated by the opposition. He apologises for the unnecessary controversy which is distracting him from the important job of governing the state.

The media is coerced into pulling the story and not discussing it anymore, but it continues to spread—the state elections are looming, so the timing is particularly significant. There are demonstrations across the state, fomented by the opposition party. Social media keeps the fire burning. Within his own party, members begin plotting against him. After days of tough negotiations, Nanjundaswamy is finally forced to resign as chief minister. At the press conference where he makes the announcement, he concludes by protesting his innocence yet again. 'If I am found guilty, I will hang myself at Freedom Park,' he declares. Sadly for him, nobody believes a word he says.

Archana was not sure what would happen when she dropped the recordings, but as she watches the events play out over the next few days, she notices that after being abandoned by his party colleagues, Nanjundaswamy is leaning more and more on Ajay and Palani. He is clearly furious that his chances of being re-elected as the chief minister are fast fading. But he is not going to go down without a fight. He is determined to rehabilitate himself with the party leaders and get back into the race. After all, this is his whole life. But first, he needs to find out who leaked those recordings.

Perhaps a political rival has planted bugs in his office. But a thorough scan reveals nothing. This is puzzling. By a process of elimination, it becomes evident that the only constant in all the meetings that have been recorded and shared is Ajay. But Ajay has been with him for over thirty-five years. First as a close friend and then as his political assistant. In return, he has been very well looked after and has become an independently wealthy man thanks to Nanjundaswamy. He has absolutely no reason to turn on him. Also, there is nothing in his recent behaviour to suggest that he has anything to do with the leaks. But it does no harm to be sure.

One Tuesday morning, during their daily briefing, when Ajay leaves the room for a moment, Nanjundaswamy checks his phone and discovers a bunch of recordings of various meetings where he had made inflammatory statements. The four leaked recordings are among them.

The discovery shocks him; it's a betrayal he least expected, by one of his closest associates. Like his own brother had stabbed him brutally in the back. Obviously, someone has got to Ajay.

By the time Ajay returns to the meeting, Nanjundaswamy has worked himself into a rage. He rises from his chair and grabs Ajay by the collar. Before Ajay can react, a stinging slap lands on one cheek, then the other. This is followed by blows to his face and vicious kicks to the stomach. In his fury, Nanjundaswamy picks up a chair and smashes it down on Ajay's head. Ajay falls to the ground, bleeding from his nose and mouth. His arm looks like it's broken. And still Nanjundaswamy does not stop.

'You snake. You traitor. You bastard. I picked you up from nowhere and brought you here and this is how you repay me. I'll destroy you and your family. Just wait. You won't find a place to live anywhere in this state, in this country. You are done!'

Ajay weakly tries to protect himself while trying to understand what Nanjundaswamy is so furious about. He had left the room for just a few minutes. What could have happened?

Hearing the sounds, other staff members come running into Nanjundaswamy's room. Seeing Ajay on the floor, injured and bleeding, a couple of men hold Nanjundaswamy back while two others help Ajay up.

'Take this traitor away. I don't want to see his face again.'

'Sir, what have I done? Why are you so angry?'

'Don't pretend!' Nanjundaswamy picks up Ajay's phone and plays one of the recordings.

'Sir, sir …'

'I don't want to hear any more of your stories. Get out!'

Nanjundaswamy turns his back on Ajay, still seething, and dials a number. 'Palani, I want to see you now. No, I don't want to hear any excuses. Come immediately.'

He sits back and thinks for a moment, then logs into his various accounts. Ajay is the one who manages every one of them as per Nanjundaswamy's instructions. At first glance, everything seems fine. But as he scrolls down, he sees that there are some random transfers to Ajay's accounts. Five lakh rupees here, ten lakh rupees there. Nothing so big that it would stand out, but none of these are transactions that Nanjundaswamy has authorised.

Nanjundaswamy is dumbfounded by Ajay's betrayal. He has never withheld anything from him—in fact, he has granted his every wish. The only time they disagreed was over a piece of land Ajay had wanted regularised for his brother-in-law several months prior. Nanjundaswamy had appeased Ajay then with a seat in an elite medical college for his niece, but it looks like he nursed the grudge till he could act on it.

It does not for a moment occur to Nanjundaswamy that there is indeed a conspiracy behind the leaks, but the person behind it is not his closest associate but someone he has not even thought of in years.

## 14

In the following days, gossip about Nanjundaswamy and Ajay's altercation spreads like wildfire. The press features stories of Ajay's rise and fall, along with theories that seek to explain why he had released the recordings. Perhaps some other political party had put him up to it, or maybe it was his own party, wishing to prop up someone else as a chief ministerial candidate. Several of Nanjundaswamy's political rivals find themselves subjects of speculation.

Ajay, however, remains silent. He chooses to focus his attention on getting back his health and reputation. Several politicians approach him, wanting to benefit from his knowledge of Nanjundaswamy's political and business affairs, but he refuses to divulge anything.

Meanwhile, Palani becomes Nanjundaswamy's closest ally, joining him for meetings, interviews and official tours. The leaked recordings soon recede from public memory. The media drops the story because they need to stay in Nanjundaswamy's good graces in case he becomes chief minister again. In a few short weeks, the story of him beating up his assistant also fades from the news altogether.

Ajay may have been sidelined, but neither he nor Nanjudaswamy have been nullified, as Archana had hoped they would be. She needs another plan.

## 15

### Ajay Naik, Former Aide to Chief Minister Nanjundaswamy, Shot Dead

In a horrendous incident in the peaceful Whitefield suburb, Ajay Naik, an erstwhile confidant of CM Nanjundaswamy, was brutally slain in a hail of bullets.

Local law enforcement reported that Naik had just finished shopping at the local grocery store when two masked assailants on a motorbike opened fire on him with nine shots—six of which struck their target.

Inspector Rupa Madan from the Whitefield police station noted that they were actively scouring nearby CCTV footage in hopes of apprehending those responsible for the heinous crime.

Nanjundaswamy said, 'I am shocked to hear that Ajay is no more. While we used to be close partners for over thirty years, these last few months, he had changed. He betrayed me by making those fake recordings and releasing them to the media. Most probably at the behest of my political enemies. And now that the task is done, they have eliminated him. It's very sad. My condolences to his family.'

The police are still investigating this shocking murder.

---

Comfortably seated in his living room, a cup of hot coffee at hand, Nanjundaswamy smiles as he reads the news. No one crosses Nanjundaswamy without consequences. Not even Ajay.

In her bedroom at the other end of town, in JP Nagar, Archana smiles too, reading the same article. This is an unexpected bonus, even if Nanjundaswamy has survived.

Four down, three to go.

# 16

Archana is becoming increasingly anxious about completing her mission. Every moment till she completes her mission is a moment away from Shalini. Janet keeps pressing her to reveal Shalu's location so she can bring her back and Archana keeps brushing her off saying, 'It's not yet time.'

Archana spends a good part of her day trying to come up with a new plan to deal with Nanjundaswamy since the old one has failed. The father and son duo are still firmly in place and on their way to being rehabilitated. It seems like nothing matters in politics; some people can commit any kind of crime and still be elected to power. Nanjundaswamy clearly demonstrates this reality.

What more can she do?

Archana returns to the secure folder where her plans have been laid out, a sudden wave of hopelessness washing over her. Nanjundaswamy seems almost untouchable given the position and the power he possesses. It makes her sick to think that someone who has committed so many wrongs can still take his place among the political elite.

Scrolling through page after page of documents, emails and photographs, Archana looks for something—anything—that she can use against Nanjundaswamy or Palani.

## 17

Day after day, little by little, Archana continues to piece together Nanjundaswamy's business empire. Every bank account, location and password. The ebb and flow of money over the days and weeks. In the past few months, she has tracked seven accounts in different parts of the world.

Each of these seven accounts deals with different parts of his empire. Three are for his property deals in the UK and Dubai. One for firearms, one for drugs. Two more for permits issued in India but with collections made abroad.

And then he has two accounts in India, which are modest and clean. One is a joint account with his wife, into which he transfers ten lakh rupees every month for home expenses. The other is a single account where his compensation as chief minister as well as other legal income from rents and businesses stream in. These are the ones accounted for, and on which he pays taxes. Of course, these bank accounts reflect only a small portion of his income. There is always a flurry of cash coming and going from his home, delivered by his driver to a few trusted aides. Telegram messages code these arrivals and departures.

Fortunately for Archana, Nanjundaswamy is old school when it comes to many things and writes down all his passwords on a notes application on his phone.

At the end of six months, she has succeeded in plotting the flow of money with reasonable accuracy. She understands that the oil that lubricates the political machinery is cash. The more the cash, the better it all works. Nanjundaswamy is a master at raising and using cash. Perhaps to take him out of the equation fully, this is where she will need to strike. Thanks to her daily vigilance, she has managed to figure out which day of the week to target in order to cause the maximum damage and attract the least attention.

She had failed at her earlier attempt to bring Nanjundaswamy down. This time, she will strike at the source of Nanjundaswamy's power: his stash of money.

## 18

It has been a month since Ajay's murder.

Palani has been in Paris for a week, on holiday with his wife and son. Ever since Ajay's departure, Nanjundaswamy has been relying far more on him, and that's not something Palani himself is happy with. While he likes the trappings of politics, he does not like the actual politicking itself. It's a lot of work. Meeting people of all sorts, most of whom want some favour or the other from him. In exchange for a lot of money, no doubt, but still, it's exhausting.

Besides, the sudden demise of Samir and Ahmed has left him feeling lonely. They were his closest friends from his school days, the three of them bonded by the many crimes they committed together, over the years. To lose them both on the same day was devastating.

He needed a break from it all, and that's why the flight to Paris, his designer wife's favourite city. She loves going to the galleries and is working on a partnership with a designer there to help boost her brand in India.

Back in Bangalore, it is around 7 p.m. when, using an anonymous VPN, Archana logs into Nanjundaswamy's Cayman Islands bank accounts and, one by one, moves a large portion of the money out, transferring it all to the Prime Minister's Relief Fund in India. He will never be able to get this money back, no matter what he tries. She leaves a reasonable amount behind to help investigators when the next part of the plan is set in motion.

Next, she crafts a message containing details of the various cash vaults holding Nanjundaswamy's vast horde of cash. Her note mentions estimated amounts, locations and passwords, and also includes details of each of the bank accounts in the Cayman Islands. And finally, the download of the Telegram group statement tracking the movement of cash, in and out. When she is done, she reads it through carefully, making sure every detail is correct, then hits 'send' to three different numbers.

The first recipient is Tara Chandrashekhar, a political journalist who is at the forefront of the anti-Nanjundaswamy camp. Almost every day, there is an article by her on any one of his many misdeeds. Nanjundaswamy has tried to silence her with money, threats and direct intimidation, but she has refused to back down.

The second person to receive the mail is the leader of the opposition, Rahul Krishna. An idealistic man in his forties who is bent on reforming the way politics is done in the state, he has sparred very often with Nanjundaswamy, in the Vidhana Soudha and outside.

The final recipient is DGP Varma.

Her task complete, Archana logs off the VPN, turns off all the other subroutines and erases from her laptop all possible traces of her actions. Then she disconnects from the internet and shuts down her laptop.

She stretches out in bed, physically exhausted by the hours spent hunched over the laptop, and closes her eyes. She is too wired to sleep. And she can't stop thinking about the repercussions of what she has just done. For herself, and for Palani and Nanjundaswamy. But it's out of her control now. If this does not work, she is done. There's nothing left in her armoury. Nanjundaswamy would have won, again. And she might well have to pay the price of discovery.

If she succeeds, however, she hopes that Shalu will forgive her and they can make peace with each other. Hopefully, Shalu can be convinced that all those years back, her parents were not trading their silence for a bag of cash.

Before she knows it, it's dawn and her phone is ringing. 'Turn on your TV,' Janet says. 'I'm coming down now.'

Archana sits up, her heart thumping. She grabs the remote and switches on the TV, then rushes to open the door.

When she returns to her living room, there's chaos on the television screen. Videos of police raids on Nanjundaswamy's and Palani's homes are playing on loop. Apparently, over 150 crore rupees of unaccounted cash have been found in all. It has been seized and taken away in trucks under the watchful eyes of the media. Details of Nanjundaswamy's overseas bank accounts are being shown on every channel.

The journalists and television anchors seem to be having the time of their life. For years they have been at the receiving end of Nanjundaswamy's vitriol. For once the shoe is on the other foot and they feel no fear. All his past crimes, his treatment of women, his son's expensive habits are described in lurid detail for the public to consume. There is a lot to make sense of still, but it is clear, as one of the TV anchors puts it, that this man is evil incarnate.

The new set of revelations, coming on top of the leaked recordings, leaves the party with no choice but to suspend him. The Enforcement Directorate and CBI have already announced that they are filing cases against him for keeping money in undeclared foreign accounts.

Everyone in his party distances themselves from him. National-level leaders issue statements denouncing him and his style of politics. As expected, Najundaswamy claims that he has been framed, despite the volume of evidence against him. This time, though, there are no takers for his theory.

There are crowds outside Nanjundaswamy's house and effigies are being burnt. He is remanded to judicial custody. And just like that, his house of cards collapses.

Rahul Krishna, the opposition leader, is on various news channels talking about the need for change and for bringing Nanjundaswamy's style of violent, corruption-led politics to an end. No one seems to disagree.

Tara Krishnaswamy goes to town with her coverage of Nanjundaswamy. Not just the arrests, but many backstories about the victims, and various crimes committed by the politician and his former sidekick, Ajay. Palani's name features often, with details of his criminal activities.

Archana is both shell-shocked and delighted. It has all happened so quickly. She did expect that there would be a fallout from the information she shared. But the speed of Nanjundaswamy's fall is breathtaking.

Of course, this is politics, so anything can happen, but everything she is hearing on the news suggests that Nanjundaswamy will not be back for a long time.

Janet stands beside her as they watch Nanjundaswamy's empire being dismantled. Her eyes are full and she makes no attempt to wipe the tears away. This is the man who took Prasad away from her. This is the man who made her life a living hell.

'It's over,' she whispers, turning to Archana, her body heaving with sobs.

That's when the last sentence in a news bulletin catches Archana's attention. 'Palani Nanjundaswamy, who is currently in Paris, has cut short his holiday and is on his way back to be with his father in these very trying times. The police await his arrival for further investigations.'

## 19

## Dubai Police Arrest Son of Former Chief Minister

Palani Nanjundaswamy, son of disgraced former chief minister S. Nanjundaswamy, has been arrested in Dubai on suspicion of indulging in child pornography. The local police said that they have uncovered a significant cache of images on his phone and browser history which violate the Emirates's strict laws and regulations against child pornography.

The United Arab Emirates does not show any leniency towards illegal content involving minors, with a fine of at least 4,00,000 Dirhams (approximately ₹80 lakh) and a minimum of six months' imprisonment mandatory for any individual found guilty. Though Palani Nanjundaswamy pleaded innocence, the damning evidence proved otherwise.

The Indian embassy has stated that they respect the local laws, and that Indian citizens must always abide by them. India, too, is known to take a firm stand against offences related to child pornography and metes out severe punishment for the same.

It should be noted that jails in Dubai are reported to be among the most brutal on earth; beatings, rapes, overcrowding and insufferable filth are just some of the conditions endured by inmates there.

## 20

'Hello?' Janet frowns at the phone that is flashing an unknown number.

'Aunty Janet?' The voice is soft and tentative.

And just like that, the years melt away.

No one in the whole world calls her Aunty Janet, except …

'Shalu? Is that you?'

'Yes, Aunty Janet.'

'How are you, my darling? Where are you, Shalu? We've gone mad waiting to see you or hear from you!'

'I … I am not very far, Aunty Janet. Back then, I was so scared I didn't know what to do. So, I just hid from everyone. I am sorry. There was too much going through my mind. But I am in a better place now, I think.'

There is a pause, then she continues haltingly, 'Aunty Janet, I need to ask you a question.'

'Of course, Shalu. Ask whatever you want. And then I am coming to get you.'

'Is Amma still in jail or is she out? Do you know?'

'Archana is out, darling. For almost a year now. She's staying in the same building as I am. We're even working together.'

'Oh …'

'Yes, dearest. She has been longing to see you, but it's like some fear holds her back; the fear that you will judge her for something she hasn't done. As if you would believe that your own mother could be a murderer! Still, I know how much she prays for your forgiveness and how much it will mean to her if you accept her. She has been crying silently every night, wondering how you are and hoping you are well. So much has happened to all of us.'

'I realise that, Aunty. I'm not a baby anymore. I understand a lot more now than I did back then.'

'Have you been following the news, Shalu? Najundaswamy and his goons have been arrested. Finally!'

'Yes, I heard the news. That's when I gathered the courage to call you. No one here knows that I am speaking to you. How is Prasad Uncle? I miss his punny jokes so much.'

'I am sorry, my baby. Prasad Uncle died a few years ago. It's a long story. I'll tell you when we meet.'

'Oh no, Aunty. I'm sorry. I should have been in touch earlier,' Shalu says tearfully.

'When can we see you?'

'Not yet, Aunty. I think I know what Amma means. I'll wait till she is ready. You have my number. Just call me before you come. I'm almost afraid to hope the day will come soon. I've been so scared about everything.'

'Don't be scared anymore, my darling. We'll start again, together. Can I tell Archu you called?' Janet asks. 'I have to tell her.'

'I guess so.'

As soon as Shalini says goodbye, Janet gets on the phone to Archana.

'Archu, you'll never believe who called.'

'Who? I know no one anymore,' Archana replies, her mind elsewhere.

'Shalu. She just called, Archu. You know what this means. She's ready to meet you. Now it's up to you!'

Archana feels the joy bubbling up from deep inside her. 'I think I'm ready now,' she says slowly. 'How about tomorrow?'

'Ok, I'll hang on somehow till tomorrow. Can't wait to see how our little Shalu has grown. Oh, when I heard that voice on the phone, my heart just broke into a million pieces. So many years by herself. In some strange place. Oh, Archana. Shalu is all we have.'

'Yes. I just pray that she'll forgive me for everything.'

'I'll beat her into forgiveness,' says Janet, and they both laugh.

## 21

The next day dawns bright and sunny. Good for the long drive to Coonoor. They plan to leave after a leisurely breakfast so they can reach by 4 p.m., when Shalini is likely to have finished work.

Just then, the doorbell rings.

'Who can it be?' Janet wonders aloud as she goes to open the door.

'Good morning, madam.'

'DGP Varma? What are you doing here so early in the morning?'

'Can I come in? Is Mrs Gowda here? I went downstairs and rang the bell, but didn't get any response.'

'Oh, I'm sorry. Of course, please do come in. And yes, Archana is here. We're just getting ready to go out. Would you like some tea?'

'Thank you, madam. Yes, please. I would really like a cup of tea,' he replies.

Archana hears his voice and looks up, surprised. She is dressed in a crisp cotton sari, a bindi on her forehead and leather flats on her feet. She follows him with her eyes as he comes and sits across from her on the sofa.

'Good morning, Mrs Gowda. How are you?' he asks.

'I am fine, Varma. I read about Nanjundaswamy and Palani few days ago. So, yes, I feel very fine,' Archana replies, her eyes flashing.

'Ah, yes, that. Suddenly, there's so much going on around us,' Varma says, his gaze intent on her face.

'Yes, I agree, Varma. Sometimes it all feels hopeless, then suddenly justice arrives in a rush.'

'Here's your tea, DGP sir. Milk and sugar ok, I hope,' says Janet.

'Thank you, madam. Yes, so many things happening, I need tea to calm down. Do you mind if I talk to Mrs Gowda alone?'

'Oh no, not at all. But don't take too much time. We have a long drive ahead of us. Archana is finally ready to meet Shalu, you see, so we are off to Coonoor,' says Janet.

'Oh, is she now?' he asks, his eyes narrowing a little. 'I won't take much time. I can't possibly stand between a mother and daughter who are meeting after so many years.'

'Ok, I'll be in my room catching up on the news.' Janet walks out of the living room, leaving Archana and Varma together again.

'What is it, Varma?'

'Let me tell you a story and you tell me what you think, madam,' he replies.

'Fifteen years ago, there lived a very happy family. A man, a woman, and their daughter, a lovely little girl. Normal people living normal lives. Then, one day, a huge tragedy struck. Tore the family apart. The father died. The daughter went missing and the mother ended up in jail.'

'I know that story, Varma. And it's not a story. It's real. It's my life.'

'Let me finish,' he says. 'The mother goes to jail for fifteen years and then she is released. What does she do now? There's no family to go back to. Her daughter is missing. Her life, as she knew it, is over. But the criminals are still out and about. So, she decides to take revenge.

'Three boys were directly involved in the crime. Of them, two are dead now. One is in jail, in Dubai. I bet he wishes he were dead. One boy stood guard when the crime took place. He is dead too. Of the men who hid the crime and put the mother in jail, one is dead and the other is in jail, where he will be for a long time. All in the last few months, coinciding with the time the mother has been out of jail. Anything to say, Mrs Gowda?'

'It's a very good story. The crime should not have occurred in the first place. But since it did, it's right that everyone involved has got justice. Many years too late, if you ask me.'

'Yes. Curious indeed. You didn't say God gave them what they deserved,' he replies.

'Varma, in my time in jail, I learnt that sometimes God helps those who help themselves.'

'Weren't you in the mobile development space all those years ago, before the tragedy?' Varma says. Without waiting for her to respond, he continues, 'I spoke to Ramiah, the jail superintendent who recommended your early release, and he said that you are a magician when it comes to mobile phones. Apparently, you helped him solve a major problem. As you did for many others in the jail.'

He pauses, waiting for Archana to say something.

'I try and help when I can. But what does that have to do with your story?'

'Ah yes, the story. As you yourself said in the beginning, it's not a story. It's your life.'

'Varma, if you have something to say, please come out and say it. Otherwise, I'll be on my way to meet my daughter.'

'Mrs Gowda, let me tell you what's bothering me. Some coincidences don't make sense, you know. All these people were doing well—I would say, very well—just a few months back. And suddenly it all came to an end.'

'What can I say, Varma? Coincidence, I suppose.'

'I don't know about Chacko yet, but there was an odd mobile phone transaction on the Ansari bank account the day the brothers killed each other. And audio recordings were found on Ajay's phone. It was a phone tip-off that got Nanjundaswamy arrested. Palani's downfall is also linked to his mobile phone. Lots of mobile phone involvement. I find that odd. Don't you?'

'I don't know, Varma. I don't know what criminals do, or how they think. My mind doesn't work that way. I'm just an old lady trying to get by.'

'Hmm, is that so? Mrs Gowda, I don't know how you did it, but I'm sure you are involved in some way. I want you to know that I know. I want you to also know that if I get the cyber team involved, they'll be able to track data movement between the cell tower around here and those near where the crimes took place. I think they'll be able to corelate these with the time when the deaths occurred and will then have enough to start an investigation.'

'I don't know what you'll find if you investigate, Varma. But if you don't investigate, no one will know.'

Varma puts his cup down and stands up, ready to leave.

'There's one more character in my story, as you know, Mrs Gowda. IG Bhaskar. We'll be keeping an eye on him, to make sure he remains safe. I'm here to tell you to be careful as well.'

'Thank you for your advice, Varma. I'll keep that in mind.'

'Mrs Rao said you are planning to meet Shalini. That's very good to hear. I think it's time for this story to have a happy ending.'

'Thank you, and God bless you, Varma.'

He leaves the house, gently shutting the door behind him.

'What was that all about? What did he want?' asks Janet, returning to the living room as soon as she hears him depart.

'Oh, nothing. Just to talk about Nanjundaswamy and Palani. And find out how I am settling down outside the jail. Anyway, enough about him. If we leave in an hour, we'll get to Coonoor by 4 p.m., right?'

'Yes, that's about right. Let's go!'

## 22

Janet has to pull out all the stops and be at her most persuasive, but she finally gets the security guard to agree to let her and Archana enter the school. It's a beautiful low-rise building built in a rustic style, with Malabar tiles and beige stone masonry walls. A small garden in front of the building greets visitors with the scent of jasmine and rose bushes. The light fragrance drifts on the breeze that whips past the ornate curlicues carved into the small columns that frame both sides of the doorway. An elderly, stern-faced nun stands at the entrance wearing a blue sari with a white border.

'Yes, what can I do for you?' she asks, looking at the two women approaching her.

'We would like to meet Shalini,' says Janet. Archana is too nervous to say anything.

'Shalini is still in class. I am the administrator of the school. May I know what this is about?' the nun asks, continuing to stand in the way.

'I am her mother,' Archana blurts out.

'Her mother?' says the nun, looking shocked. 'But her mother …' Her voice trails away.

Janet chimes in, 'Yes, her mother was in jail for …'

'A crime she did not commit,' says a voice behind them.

Archana turns to see a pretty, short-haired young woman wearing a big smile on her face.

Her Shalini.

'Shalu.' Her voice breaks as she steps forward and opens her arms.

Shalini collapses into her mother's embrace. They hold tight to each other, laughing and crying at the same time. Then Archana turns to include Janet in their embrace, while the nun watches them with a broad smile on her face.

A few moments later, they are led by the administrator to an anteroom, its walls adorned with religious artifacts and candles flickering in every corner. Almost immediately, Sister Philomena follows them in. She is a small woman, but her presence fills the room. Her kind eyes shine with unshed tears as she walks straight up to Archana and hugs her.

All through those last years in jail, it was Sister Philomena's messages and the photographs of Shalini she shared that kept Archana going. She greets her now with a warm hug that conceals a sense of guilt and uncertainty—would the good nun regret what she did for her and for Shalu if she knew the whole truth?

'Thank you,' she says simply.

'No, thank *you*. We are blessed that Mother Mary gave us a chance to look after your daughter,' the nun replies compassionately.

Archana turns to Shalini, her eyes shining with love. 'I'm sorry, Shalu,' she says. 'For everything that happened that horrible evening, all those years ago. And for not being with you as you grew up alone. We are really blessed that you found a second home here with these beautiful people, with Sister Beatrice and Sister Philomena.'

Shalu looks at her wordlessly, as though waiting for something.

'The nightmare is over, my darling. All those people who hurt you, they've been punished for what they did,' Archana tells her.

Shalini grins then, gladly, almost mischievously. 'I know, Amma. I know. I also think I know how it happened.'

'What do you mean, you know how it happened?' asks Janet.

Archana holds Shalu's hand tightly. 'I think she means she has heard about how it all happened.'

'Yes, Aunty Janet. I've been following the news every day.'

'Shalu, I know you've built a life here and I don't want to disrupt it,' Archana says. 'We'll stay here for a few days, then go back to Bangalore. I can always come back, or you come and stay with me whenever you can.'

'Of course, Amma. School holidays are starting in three weeks. Why don't you both come here then and we'll stay in Coonoor for a while. I need my mother with me. And my favourite aunt,' she adds, smiling at Janet.

## 23

Their time with Shalini in Coonoor is everything Archana and Janet could have asked for. The mornings are spent walking and chatting, taking in the crisp air redolent of autumn leaves and wood smoke. They have breakfast together before Shalini goes to school. Then Janet and Archana spend the day with their work, often lapsing into memories of the old days and making plans for the future, while waiting for Shalini to return from school.

The days fly by. A new family, or what is left of two families, is being put together bit by bit. But the pain of Raju's and Prasad's absence is a constant. Archana's desire to meet Shalini and make up with her, as well as the need to take revenge, had temporarily shut out all thoughts of Raju. But now, every day, she is reminded of him. His quiet fortitude. His humour. His dependability. She will have to find a way to live her life on these memories.

And, of course, there is the matter of the one man she hasn't been able to deal with yet. IG Bhaskar was the one who came to talk to Raju and planted the seed of doubt while pretending to be a concerned father. From that meeting followed the series of tragedies that destroyed their lives.

No matter Varma's warning, she can't let the man get away with what he did to them, to Raju in particular. He has to pay, regardless of the consequences.

On their last afternoon in Coonoor, Archana slips away to the local internet café, her mind ticking with possibilities.

## 24

### BREAKING NEWS

ANCHOR: Good evening! I'm Deepali, for Bharat Today News. Our top story tonight: a shocking revelation involving a former

Inspector General has sent shockwaves throughout the nation.

(CUT TO IMAGES OF BHASKAR'S ARREST)

ANCHOR: In a stunning turn of events, former Inspector General Bhaskar is behind bars tonight, accused of a grave breach of national security. Authorities allege that he provided sensitive information to a Pakistani national.

(CUT TO IMAGES OF BHASKAR AND HIS PHONE)

ANCHOR: A thorough search of the former IG's phone uncovered alarming evidence, including missile blueprints and multiple images of Indian defence airports. Even more concerning were the messages indicating troop movements which were found on his device.

[CUT TO NSA RAID FOOTAGE]

ANCHOR: Acting on a tip-off, the National Security Agency (NSA) raided the former IG's home, leading to the discovery of not only sensitive data but also details of his contacts and information shared over the past few months.

(CUT TO POLICE AND MILITARY OFFICIALS STANDING OUTSIDE AN OFFICE BUILDING)

ANCHOR: The reasons behind these acts of treachery remains shrouded in mystery at this time, according to police and military personnel handling the case. An official statement from law enforcement emphasised the gravity of the situation and concluded with the resolve to 'show everyone that we will not tolerate any such betrayal of our great nation.'

The maximum possible sentence for such treasonous acts under the Official Secrets Act is life imprisonment along with a heavy fine.

The nation is left stunned by these allegations against a former high-ranking official, and as the investigation unfolds, questions about the extent of the damage caused and the motives behind this alleged act of treason remain unanswered. We will continue to follow this developing story and bring you the latest updates as they become available.

Archana looks away from the news when she hears her phone ring. She knows who it is before she sees the name on the screen. DGP Varma.

She lets it ring for a while, then disconnects. She has no intention of answering the phone or speaking to him again. That part of her life is over.

# Epilogue

## Eleven Months Later

It is a sunny day in the city of Bengaluru, no longer describable as either garden city or retirement haven. The road outside the apartment complex is already buzzing with traffic at 6 o'clock, when Archana steps out for her morning walk. She is on tenterhooks as she completes ten rounds of the block, waiting for the newspapaper vendor to arrive and chuck her the day's paper.

The previous evening, she had watched television and tracked every social media handle she could think of, to keep abreast of the impending verdict in the case relating to former CM Nanjundaswamy. She went to bed relieved but with a lingering sense of uncertainty. What if something made them change their mind? What if the verdict was overturned unexpectedly?

Somehow, seeing the news in the paper will make it real, unchangeable.

A moment later, the newspaper man is at the gate, and she is fumbling to unfold the day's *Bangalore Express*. The headline screams at her in big, bold type:

Former CM Sentenced to 15 Years in Prison.

She reads through the article, stopping to register the important points: Nanjundaswamy has been found guilty on all counts of bribery, fraud and money laundering. There is substantial evidence linking him to money deposited in multiple offshore accounts. On behalf of his client, defence attorney Shinde has announced that he will be filing an appeal in the Supreme Court. In the meantime, the former CM will serve time in Bangalore Central Jail.

'Bangalore Central Jail?'

Archana smiles as she walks back home, a spring in her step.

She must remember to call Fakii later in the day. She will be delighted.

# Author's Note

Every day there is a news report about some heinous crime that's been committed in this vast country of ours. And that's it. Unless someone famous is involved or it's particularly gruesome, think Nirbhaya, there is seldom any information about what happened next. Were the criminals arrested? Were they convicted? How is the victim's family doing? These questions almost never get answered.

One also reads stories about people being acquitted by the courts because of witnesses recanting, evidence getting misplaced, shoddy investigations and other such reasons, suggesting that those with influence were able to work their way through the system.

Finally, and perhaps naively, one often feels that such things only happen to people 'not like us'. It's usually someone who lives in a village far away, or is very rich, or from a different socioeconomic strata. Middle-class Indians in white-collar jobs live in a world largely removed from this sort of crime.

Then one day, I read the news about a young girl in Hyderabad who had been raped by six boys, including the son of an MLA. I have no idea what happened in the case, but it planted a seed in my mind for this book, bringing together the three strands I mention above.

*Redemption* is a story that attempts to show what happens to everyone involved when a terrible crime befalls a 'regular' upper middle-class family.

This is my first book. Let me know what you think at booksbyharish@gmail.com.

# Acknowledgements

Beyond family and friends, I owe my gratitude to:

Vijay Raghavan from Prayas for answering all my prison related queries. They are doing some remarkable work with women and young undertrials and those being processed by the criminal justice system, to shift them away from an environment conducive to crime or commercial sexual exploitation. Do look them up at https://www.tiss.edu/view/11/projects/prayas/.

The Westland team, led by Karthika V.K., who took personal interest in getting the book out of me and shepherding it through to the final product you hold in your hands.